D

I'd been sleeping ... blanket, which I used as a pillow. I eased it out and thumbed back the hammer. In reality, the sound was a minuscule, oiled *click*—but in the dark of night it sounded like a couple of cooking pots being slammed together.

Armando drew his boot knife. I could hear the ten inch blade slide out of its leather sheath sewn into his left boot, which left his right hand free to draw his pistol.

I didn't know any of the Indians in the area, but that didn't mean they weren't there. Then I saw the image of six dead men on the street in Burnt Rock. Each of those cowpokes had friends, relatives, maybe partners, and they'd want revenge.

Arm drew an arc on my shoulder, pointing me off to the left. I got my feet under me and duck-walked very slowly and as quietly as I could about twenty feet. I assumed Armando was doing the same think to the right, but I couldn't hear a sound from him.

All of a sudden, the place we'd been sleeping erupted dirt and stone and sand into the sky. The hollow, deep boom of at least one shotgun mixed with the sharper, quicker pistol reports. One shot— and then another—was deeper and louder than the others. One of those boys was firing a Sharps. '

Arm and I opened up on the muzzle flashes . . .

Other *Leisure* books by Paul Bagdon:

OUTLAW LAWMAN
OUTLAWS
BRONC MAN
DESERTER
PARTNERS

THE BUSTED THUMB HORSE RANCH

Paul Bagdon

Onondaga Free Library

LEISURE BOOKS NEW YORK CITY

A LEISURE BOOK®

January 2010

Published by

Dorchester Publishing Co., Inc.
200 Madison Avenue
New York, NY 10016

ISBN 10: 0-8439-6177-5
ISBN 13: 978-0-8439-6177-5
E-ISBN: 978-1-4285-0799-9

The name "Leisure Books" and the stylized "L" with design are
trademarks of Dorchester Publishing Co., Inc.

Printed in the United States of America.

10 9 8 7 6 5 4 3 2 1

Visit us online at www.dorchesterpub.com.

THE BUSTED THUMB HORSE RANCH

Chapter One

The document—that's what the circuit rider judge called it: the document—was ten or a dozen pages long, tucked neatly into a black leather folder. There were a herd of whereases, heretofores, perpetuities, and parties of the first and second parts on each page.

"I don't get it," I said.

Armando SantaMaria, my partner, poured himself another shot of whiskey, and downed it. "White-man bullsheet," he mumbled.

"It's quite simple," the judge said to me, ignoring Arm. "You've inherited a thousand acres, a house, a barn, and six thousand dollars from Hiram Ven Gelpwell, deceased."

"But I don't even know . . ."

"Whether or not you know or don't know matters not a twittle. Suffice it to say that he was an . . . uhh . . . paramour of your mother's. He felt responsible, for some reason, for you."

"Where is theese land?" Armando asked. "And where is the six thousand dollars?"

The judge looked at Armando the way a new bride would look at a squished cockroach on her piece of wedding cake. "The land is in West Texas," the judge said. "I have here a certified bank check made payable to Jake Walters in the amount mentioned."

"*Bueno*," Arm chuckled. "We can drink up the dollars an' raise prairie dogs on the rocks an' sand. Or maybe the rattlers an' scorpions, no?"

The judge ignored Arm. "The land is good for the area," he said, "and there's a year-around stream. It's a tad slight in the summer, but it never goes dry. The pasture is sparse but it'll support some beef." He took a loose map from the folder and handed it to me. The land I apparently owned was outlined in heavy ink. It looked big. The nearest town was Hulberton.

"What's the town like?" I asked.

"I was through there once a few years ago," the judge said. "It's much like any West Texas cattle and Farmington town—a decent mercantile, two saloons, a blacksmith and livery shop, a bank, a small hotel with a restaurant, a house of soiled doves—that's about it. There's a railroad spur not too far away and that's what brings in the business—cowpokes with cash at the end of a drive."

"What do I have to do?" I asked.

"Sign here—and here—and here—and here. Then I hand the bank draft to you and our business is concluded." The judge handed me a pen and a small ink pot. I signed in the places indicated and the judge handed over the draft and a copy of the whole mess.

Arm and me now had a prairie dog, rattlesnake, and scorpion ranch—and $6,000.

"Ain't that somethin'," I said. "This here piece of paper is worth six thousand dollars."

"Maybe might could be," Armando said. "Me, I think it's white man's scribbling an' will find trouble for us."

I looked across the table at my partner. He was all Mexican, that was obvious, from the wet sand color of his skin to the deep, unfathomable chestnut of his eyes. He wasn't what one would refer to as handsome; he had deep acne craters from the pox on his face as a youth, there was an elevated four-inch scar running from his forehead, through his left eyebrow and onto his cheek, and his nose had been broken and not set several more times than once. His mustache ran shaggily over his upper lip, down each side of his mouth, and then beyond his jaw a couple of inches to dangle freely.

"What you gawkin' at?" he asked. His voice was a whiskey, tobacco, and cinders sound that grated on the listener's ears.

"Your beauty, Arm. At times it purely stuns me."

He grinned, showing a wonderful set of white, straight teeth so many Mexicans are blessed with. "Is true," he said. "Let's drink much cerveza," he said. "We celebrate theese ranch, no?"

"It's *beer*, you damned fool," I said. "You're not a campesino in some adobe hut—you're in America. We drink beer, not cerveza."

Armando stood, still grinning, and clutched his genitals with his right hand. "Here is your America, gringo. You fight a good an' just war an' get your asses shot off. The bes' part of your country couldn't fight worth a damn, an' now your South, it is nothing, the remains of a campfire."

Armando and I had been partners for better than twenty years. We'd both run off from our homes—my father was a drunken oaf of a sod-buster, and Arm's mother was a whore and he had no idea who his father may have been. We met near a long curve of railroad tracks close to the Tex-Mex border, waiting to hop a train. We joined up and haven't been apart since.

Sometimes it happens that way, between boys or between full-grown men. There's something there that holds them together—makes them partners. I don't know what that force is, but I'm right glad it exists.

"Let's drink lots of cerveza," I said. "And talk about our ranch."

We commenced to do just that.

We were roughly 400 miles from Hulberton and our ranch and had no real idea what lay between us and our destination beyond sand, mesquite, scraggly desert pines, little water, and wandering gangs of screwups from both sides of the war who were as crazy as shithouse rats and blood-thirsty, to boot.

The distance didn't much bother us; we'd covered more ground than that either running from the law or headed in one direction or another simply to see what was there. Rabbit isn't a bad feed, although a man grows tired of it when eating it twice a day for long periods of time.

We figured we'd best cash the bank draft, provision up at the mercantile, and set out. The bank in this little town, Burnt Rock, was small, as was the town itself. We had to talk to the chief officer, a turtlelike old fellow whose face showed he didn't like most people and, in particular, didn't like drifters who smelled like beer barrels and looked like they didn't have a penny between them. The fact that Arm was a Mex didn't cheer him up any, either.

"What is it I can do for you?" he asked. A little plaque on his desk said his name was ALVIN L. TERHUNE.

"Well, I'll tell ya, Al," I said. "We want to cash this here draft." I handed it to him.

"You'll refer to me as Mr. Terhune," he said, his voice as frigid as a West Texas winter.

"I'll refer to you as the tooth fairy if I care to," I said. "Just cash the damn draft."

He began to reply when Armando released a truly thunderous belch that was loud enough to rattle the windowpanes.

"You swine!" Terhune snapped. "You can't . . ."

Arm grinned. "Ain't much I'd rather do with a ol' woodchuck like you than swing you by your tail an' whack your ugly head 'gainst a rock. Now, you do like Jake says an' we'll saddle up an' haul ass."

Terhune's hand trembled as he inspected the draft. Evidently, it was the sort of thing he'd have to cash if Satan himself came walking in with it. He pushed his chair from his desk and stood. I noticed that Arm took a step to the side and let the fingertips of his right hand just barely touch the bone grips of the holstered Colt .45 he had tied with latigo lower on his leg than a cowhand would. He actually thought the old codger was going to draw on us. I laughed.

"Get the money 'fore you get my partner all sweaty an' bothered, Al," I said. "All fifties'll be just fine."

Terhune glared at us for a moment longer and then stomped off toward the line of three tellers behind little windows across the room.

"You ever notice how silly a little man with a fat ass looks?" I asked Arm.

"*Sí.*"

The safe must have been in a room behind the tellers. Terhune used a key to open the door of the room, went inside, and locked the door behind himself. For a few moments there was no sound. Then we heard the door unlock. Terhune emerged with a cloth sack in one hand and relocked the door. He walked to his desk and dropped the bag on it. "Count it," he said.

"No need," Arm said jovially. "You ain't got the eggs to try to cheat us." I picked up the sack and liked the heft of it. We left the bank.

I've always liked a good mercantile, and the one in Burnt Rock was the best I'd been in for a long time. Everything was neatly arranged, the glass of the cases glistened, and the scent inside the place was a delightful mixture of leather, wood, penny candy, fabric, apples, and the steel of plows and other farm implements. We walked up and down the aisles, checking out the saddles, bits, and bridles, passed by the patent medicines, dresses, and ladies' hats, looked over the rifles and pistols in a glass-fronted case, and went back to the main counter. An ol' gent dressed in a suit with shoes shiny enough to hurt if you looked at them in the sun gave us a large sack.

We picked up maybe six pounds of beef jerky, 1,000 rounds of Remington .45 ammunition, four quarts of whiskey, a couple pounds of tobacco and several books of rolling papers, four canteens apiece, and a Buck knife that caught Arm's fancy. That filled the sack; I went back and got another one. We bought a half dozen cans of peaches in heavy syrup, a dozen or so apples, and a box of cigars. I tried on a tooled leather vest that was the nicest piece of goods I'd ever seen and left my ol' vest in a trash barrel.

We didn't need anything in terms of sad-dlery—we both rode Texas-made double-rig working saddles and used low-port bits, and everything was in good shape. We picked up a can of neat's-foot oil and a couple cans of Hoppe's gun oil, and that was it.

When we put everything on the counter we saw it'd be impossible to stuff everything into our saddlebags.

"We need a pack animal," I said.

Arm nodded. "I'll go to the livery an' buy one—you get us a pack rig."

I reached into the money bag and gave a few bills to my partner. He stuffed them in his pocket without looking at them. We both knew that it was our money, not mine. That's the way we did things.

I picked out a pack rig. If a fella knew what he was doing, a mule or horse could be loaded securely with a single, long length of good rope. Neither Arm nor I had that skill, and the leather rig was a whole lot easier on the animal.

The mercantile owner was running a tally on a

sheet of paper, and the more he added, the broader his smile became. He offered me a free cigar, which I accepted, and was just putting a match to, when raucous laughter penetrated the mercantile from the street. "Hey, Pancho," a drunken voice bellowed, "why not trade your ma an' your sister for a saddle for that nag?" The laughter rose again, swelled, took on the sharp edge of mockery.

"Damn," I said, and set my cigar on the counter and headed for the door.

There were six men—cowhands, from the looks of them—mostly drunk, in a scraggly line facing Armando and a ribby bay mare he had on a lead line.

I left the mercantile and walked to a spot about ten feet to Arm's left. "Partner," I said quietly. Sneaking up on a man in the position Arm was in could easily buy a fella a hole on boot hill.

Arm dropped the lead rope and let his hands hang to his sides. I carried a Colt .45, too, and wore it as Arm wore his—low, tied to my leg, ready for action.

Three of the cowpokes had stepped forward, a yard in front of their friends. One carried a lever action 30.30 and the other two wore holstered handguns.

"Maybe you boys better back off an' grab another drink," I said. "If you don't, most—maybe all—of you are going down hard and going down dead."

Jagged laughter ran through the men. The one with the rifle cranked the action, chambering a round.

"You and the beaner gonna shoot us up?" the rifleman asked. "You gonna kill us dead?" The laughter covered my few quiet words to Armando. "I got the rifle an' the two to the left."

Armando nodded.

The rifleman seemed to be the leader. I thought that if I took him down fast, the others may turn tail. It was far from a sure thing, but I guessed it was worth a try.

The barrel of the 30.30 rose toward me. I drew and blew a hole in the man's throat. He took a step back and then collapsed like a sack of grain tossed from a wagon. The two men to his side were scrambling to draw their pistols. I fired twice: one slug entered through one cowpoke's right eye, the other in the middle of his friend's chest. I heard Arm's .45 bark two or three—or maybe four times, he fired so rapidly, it was hard to tell—and his three targets were splayed on the street, their blood soaking into the dirt and grit.

Arm and I both reloaded our pistols before we reholstered them. We always do. It's a good habit to get into. There aren't many worse sounds than squeezing a trigger in a bad situation and hearing a click instead of a bang.

" 'Bout time to leave Burnt Rock," I said.

"Sí," Armando answered. The packhorse had run into an alley between buildings and Arm went after him.

I went back into the mercantile to settle up our bill and to retrieve the cigar I'd left on the counter. "How's the law around here?" I asked.

The store owner was white faced and a little shaky. He'd obviously watched the action from the window. He stuttered slightly as he spoke. "There isn't any law just now," he said. "Our sheriff got gunned down two or three weeks ago an' we can't find nobody who cares to fill the job. Deputy was killed, too. Goddamn army is out chasin' Injuns."

I nodded. "Now, how about finishing adding up our charges?"

He went back to his piece of paper and his nub of a pencil, his lips moving as he ran the sums. "It's . . . uhh . . . a bit high," he said, as if he were apologizing.

"That's not a big surprise," I said. "C'mon—what do you need to square us up?"

"Well," he said, "it's $48.52, all told."

I handed him a fifty. His face lit up like I'd handed him the key to paradise. "Keep the change," I said. A thought struck me. "Damn," I said. "We forgot coffee. Add in twenty pounds." I had a scrunched-up ten-dollar bill in my pocket and dropped it on the counter. "That'll cover it, no?"

"Oh, yessir—I can sell you twenty pounds for that and give you change."

"Give us the coffee and keep the change."

Armando had tied the packhorse to the rail outside. We fitted the rig to the horse and loaded up. There was some weight to our purchases, but not so much that it'd wear down the horse. He'd carried before; we could see the places where the straps had rested on his hide.

We led the horse down to the livery to pick up our own mounts. Arm's horse was a tall, broad-chested, big-assed short-horse type, completely black except for two white socks in front and a snip of white on his snout. Mine was an Appaloosa that stood a bit more than fifteen hands and was faster than a bolt of lightning and about as dumb as a shovel. He'd go all day and all night, though, without a complaint, and gunfire from his back barely caused him to prick his ears. Arm hadn't had his black too long and the horse could get jittery at times, but Arm could always ride him down without a problem. We figured I should hook up with the packhorse. I took a wrap around my saddle horn with the lead rope and we rode on out of Burnt Rock, headed east and slightly north. We gave the bodies in the street a wide berth. The best of horses got antsy when they got the scent of human blood.

We filled our canteens at the livery pump, let the horses have a last suck at the trough there, and set out.

There were men peering through windows and gathered in alleys as we left town. Before long, the dead men's boots, guns, cash, hats, and anything else of value would be gone and the boot-hill man would have six half-dressed corpses to plant in unmarked graves.

We rode until just about dark, each smoking cigars and having the occasional suck on a whiskey bottle. Early on there was some nipping and screwing around among the horses, but that calmed right down. The pack animal figured out that the other two horses ran the show and decided it was easier to live with that than to have chunks of hide and hair chewed out of him.

I guess maybe I didn't mention that it was early July when all this took place. The sun hung in the sky ten or eleven hours a day, like a probing, blinding, maniacal eye. It was the sort of wringing-wet, oppressive heat that caused problems that otherwise wouldn't have taken place. Good dogs—cattle dogs—tore into their owners—or their owner's kids, for no reason at all. Men who'd been friends for years traded punches and rolled over one another biting, gouging, and kicking in the spilled beer and damp sawdust and blood of saloon floors. Kids were listless and surly, ignored their chores, sassed their folks.

I don't know that it's really possible to get used to the sort of heat we were experiencing, but Arm and I had done a good deal of traveling in it, and we did generally all right. For instance, a few years ago, I'd somehow developed the habit of humming as we plodded along. It was a tuneless sound and why I did it or where it came from, I have no idea. Arm listened for a few days and then said, "If you don't queet that buzzing, I'll tear your stupid head off an' stick it up your ass."

I quit humming.

We made camp just before dark. We hobbled the horses, gave them each a Stetson full of water, which wasn't enough but was a lot better than no water at all. Armando and I each had a can of peaches in syrup, a few solid hits of whiskey, and, when our coffee was boiling, slurped down a couple cupfuls each.

"This ain't Arbuckles'," Arm commented. "Don't have much flavor to it."

"Don't drink it then," I said. "Next time, you

pick out the brand. Far as I'm concerned it's all the same coffee in different sacks." Arm grumbled something I couldn't hear, which was fine with me.

Before our small mesquite fire had burned out completely, we were both asleep.

Morning slides in real early in a West Texas summer. I started the fire and put the coffee on in near dark while Arm checked over the horses. We loaded up our packhorse, saddled our own animals, drank a pot of coffee, and were traveling before the huge brass disc of the sun had cleared the horizon.

"Be good to cross water today," Arm said. "Four canteens don't go far between three horses and two men." Neither of us drank—the only water we used was that for the coffee. The rest went into our hats for the horses.

Long before noon the sun was enough to bring the rattlesnakes out, seeking not prey but warm rocks to rest upon, soaking up the heat. Every so often one of us would draw and nail a rattler, especially the big ones—and they got big out there. Six-footers were fairly common and eight-footers not completely rare. Sonsabitches were as big around as a strong man's forearm. I heard-tell that a man can tell the age of a rattler by the number of buttons on its tail, but Arm said that ain't the case. He said there's a new button every time the snake sheds, and that could be four or five times a year. I'm not so sure about that, but it wasn't worth arguing about.

After four or so hours of riding our shirts were soaked through with sweat and stuck to our backs and chests. We reined in and pulled the cinches to let the horses breathe a bit, but we had no water to offer them. After maybe twenty or thirty minutes we cinched up and went on. The afternoon lasted forever. Our horses plodded along, heads much lower than usual, often scraping their toes in the sand and dirt, indicating how fatigued they were.

Arm's eyes were better than mine. "Up there—I see some scrub an' maybe a few desert pine. Mus' be water there, even should we have to dig for it." Moments later all three of the horses' heads perked up and their nostrils widened as they caught the scent of the mud or water or whatever was there.

There were a few scraggly-assed desert pines in a clumsy half circle and some buffalo grass that showed a tiny bit of green. The horses wanted to run and we let them.

The water pocket was about the size and shape of a good-size trough, maybe a foot deep. It was sulphur water but there rodent tracks all around it, so it wasn't poisonous. Arm vaulted off his horse into the muck and water and so did I. The horses waded in and began to suck hard. After a few minutes we had to drag them out still thirsty, wait ten minutes or so, and let them have at it again. Arm and I drank as much as we wanted and then filled the canteens.

I'll tell you what: there ain't many things that put out the stench warm sulphur water does, and both Armando and I puked up some of it later, but it tasted as good as fresh cream when we gulped it down. The animals didn't have any problems with it, though.

We decided to make camp there for the night. The hobbled horses could graze through the buffalo grass and stumble over to the water when they cared to. Arm went out and returned in fifteen minutes with a couple of nice jackrabbits. I skinned them and cleaned them out and we chowed down. Then we settled back with cigars and a bottle of booze.

"Ya know," I said, "this ranch is a perfect chance for us to see if what we've been yapping about for years can really work."

"Is true. I have the same thought. Maybe we run a few head of beef, but make our business the breeding of the fine horses, no?"

"Finest ranch an' working horses," I said. "I know we can do it, Arm, if we can gather up the right stock."

"Lotsa mustangs aroun' there."

"Yeah—mostly jugheads an' tanglefoots, though. But still, you're right, there must be some good ones."

"Plus, we have plenty dollars if we need to buy one we can't steal—from another ranch, I mean."

"We'll need good fences an' corrals."

"Sí. Ain' no problem, though."

I took a good, long pull at the bottle and settled back, enjoying the heat in my gut and the way the booze kind of whisked away how much work we'd have to do for a very unsure outcome.

"Look," I said, as if I were explaining our idea for the first time, "a cowpoke on a drive needs a string of five or so horses. Most are no damned good—half broke, stupid, lazy, an' clumsy with the conformation of a damn goat. With the right breeding we can bring along strong, smart, hardy horses that a cowhand won't need more than a pair of, no matter how long the drive. We can get big bucks for such horses."

"We already got the big bucks an' a ranch to boot," Arm said. He chuckled a bit. "You an' me, we want to make this horse even should we starve to death, no? Is our dream, no?"

"Yeah. *Es verdad.*"

"Right." Arm traded my Spanish for English. "Is true."

We kept tapping away at the whiskey, not drinking hard, but regularly—a belt every few minutes. Before long I heard Armando's breathing become quiet and slightly sibilant. He was sound asleep.

The moonlight out on a desert area such as where we were is awfully pretty. It's like a soft gossamer fog has descended to soften everything—so that there were few, if any, sharp angles or jagged terrain. I finished off the bottle, set it aside, and closed my eyes.

I saw the ranch clearly; the fences were arrow-straight and tight. The snubbing post in the center of the corral was stout and stood at attention. A coil of rope hung over the gate post. The house was freshly painted—white, of course—and its lines were true and sturdy-looking. There was a porch around the front of the place with a couple rocker-type chairs waiting to be used of an evening.

The barn was a two-story, ten-stall structure. The roof looked good and the red paint dusty but not worn away by the elements.

A bay horse stood in the corral, tearing mouthfuls from a flake of hay. He was tall—every bit of sixteen hands—with a chest like the front of a locomotive. He stood squarely and the muscles of his forelegs bulged slightly against his flesh. His tail—black, of course— swished lackadaisically at flies. His flanks were tight and perfectly formed, and not a rib showed. Very suddenly, I was standing in front of him, looking into his eyes. It was like looking into the eyes of an eagle, but without the taint of aggression an eagle would show.

The horse snorted . . .

I came awake immediately. During my sleep a thick cloud front had moved in; there was no more light than there'd be in a tomb. The snort was real, not part of my dream—and it was the snort of a horse coming upon others he didn't know: half challenge and half greeting.

I felt Arm's finger tap my shoulder three times. He must have been crouched next to me but I couldn't see him. So—there were at least three men out there, perhaps one or two more. Arm had hearing like no other man I've known and he must have heard boots scuffling in the sand.

I'd been sleeping with my Colt under my saddle blanket, which I used as a pillow. I eased it out and thumbed back the hammer. In reality, the sound was a minuscule, oiled *click*—but in the dark that night it sounded like a couple of cooking pots being slammed together.

Armando drew his boot knife. I could hear the

ten-inch blade slide out of its leather sheath sewn into his left boot, which left his right hand free to draw his pistol.

I didn't know of any hostile Indians in the area, but that didn't mean they weren't there. Then I saw the image of the six dead men on the street in Burnt Rock. Each of those cowpokes had friends, relatives, maybe partners, and they'd want revenge.

Arm drew an arc on my shoulder, pointing me off to the left. I got my feet under me and duck-walked very slowly and as quietly as I could about twenty feet. I assumed Armando was doing the same to the right, but I couldn't hear a sound from him. A bat swooped past my face, its high-pitched squeak announcing it. I damned near fired on it before I got my wits back about me.

All of a sudden, the place where we'd been sleeping erupted dirt and stone and sand into the sky. The hollow, deep boom of at least one shotgun mixed with the sharper, quicker pistol reports. One shot—and then another—was deeper and louder than the others. One of those boys was firing a Sharps.

Arm and I opened up on the muzzle flashes. It was almost too easy. I still had a round left in my pistol when the attackers were totally silent. I felt like a goddamn executioner, but I didn't see that we had a choice in the matter—those men were out for our blood and if they were stupid enough to offer us targets the way they did, it wasn't our fault.

There was no wind—not even the lightest breeze—and a thick cloud of acrid gunsmoke hung about chest level all around us. As we drew closer to the attackers the unmistakable coppery smell of fresh spilled blood melded with the gunpowder stink.

I struck a match. There were four of them, three obviously dead and the fourth, gut-shot, clutching at his stomach and moaning quietly. Bleeding out from a gut shot is no way to die. Before my match burned down, Armando put a bullet between the fellow's eyes.

"Ten lives we took this day," Armando said quietly. "Surely we'll fry in hell."

"We would have with or without the ten today," I said, but I knew what Arm was feeling because I was feeling the same thing—a weight in my chest and a profound awareness of what we'd done. There was no joy in killing for us. We protected ourselves, and we realized that. Still, the weight and the realization remained.

We walked out of the haze of the battle and settled down to await the coming of the next day. I didn't sleep and I don't think Arm did, either. It seemed like a long time, but it couldn't have been more than a couple of hours.

We stood and stretched at the very first light. The corpses were covered with flies—where the sonsabitches came from, beats me, but there they were. A half dozen vultures were circling high above us—as it got lighter they'd come lower.

The attackers' horses stood in a cluster, trying to gouge some grazing out of the dull brown buffalo grass. Armando looked them over and then unsaddled and unbridled each, dropped the gear and the ground, and slapped him on the rump.

"Nothin' there worth havin'," he said.

I picked up the Sharps from next to one of the bodies. "This is sure worth havin', though," I said. "Ever fired one?"

"No—an' I ain't gonna fire that one. That's a dead man's rifle, Jake. Is evil to take it, to use it."

"Yer ass. The Sharps is the best rifle in the world, regardless of who owned it or used it." I held the rifle to my shoulder and swept the land-scape with it. It was fairly heavy but easy to handle, and it'd had good care. I could smell gun oil on it. I plucked a round from the bandolier around the dead man's chest, chambered it, and took a vulture out of the sky as easy as spitting in the dirt.

"Shoots good—but ees still a dead man's rifle."

"That vulture didn't seem to notice the differ-ence," I said.

Armando grunted. After a moment he said, "You wan' to stand 'round here burnin' daylight or get ridin'?" In twenty or so minutes we'd filled the canteens, let the horses drink, and were on our way. The vultures were lower. Arm tried a shot with his 30.30 but missed. I blew apart the bird he'd aimed at with the Sharps, which pissed him off. He didn't say anything for quite some time, which wasn't unusual behavior for him.

Later in the day, he said, " 'Course a rifle don't know if it was owned by a dead man. It's only a damned gun an' they don't know nothing, right?" He held his hand out to me. I handed the Sharps to him. He looked it over carefully and then raised the stock to his shoulder and fired. A rab-bit so far away I couldn't see anything but a tiny brown blur exploded when the thumb-size bullet hit it, like a fountain of pink and red and gray bits and pieces.

"Damn," Arm said. "Ees good gun." He handed the rifle back to me.

We got lucky later that day. A slow, warm rain began and continued through the night and into the next day. We covered good distance. On the second day of the rain the temperature had moderated delightfully. The horses became frisky, dancing, trying to get under the bit to run. We held them in, but rode at a slow lope throughout the balance of the day.

The next day we were back to inferno temperatures and scalding sun.

"How far you think we come?" Arm asked.

"I dunno, but we did good the last couple days. I figure we're a bit better'n halfway to Hulberton."

"Shit," Arm grunted. "I thought more. Theese long ridin' is a pain in the ass, no?"

I grinned at him. "Sometimes a cigar an' a nip of red-eye helps out, *mi* amigo."

It did help out. It was hotter'n a wolf bitch in heat, but we made good distance and even crossed a large spring-fed puddle that was icy cold and as sweet as water could ever be. We drank and led the horses in and out until they'd had enough. We filled all the canteens and mounted up. It was coming dusk by then.

"We have more whiskey an' cigars, no?" Arm said.

"Sure."

He looked up at the sky. There wasn't a cloud

in sight. "We have good moonlight tonight. What say we keep on ridin'?"

"Fine idea," I said. We each lit another cigar, passed the bottle back and forth, and kept on moving. We did so well that night we rode through the next day, using the same booze an' tobacco system of travel. About midafternoon we came across a sort of small oasis, with water, a few desert pine, and some blessed shade the small trees yielded. We stripped down the horses, gave them each a hatful of water, hobbled them, and slept until the sun was rising the next morning.

We started seeing free-range cattle. These beef were never handled by man, and, in fact, most of them had probably never even seen a human. They were strong, fast, and wild as hawks. "Is our first good meal at our ranch when we get there," Arm announced, watching a longhorn standing a couple hundred yards off. He was right. I doubted that any of the free-rangers had ever seen a branding iron; they were the offspring of other free-range beef, putting them another step away from an owner. So, we had as much right to shoot and butcher one as we did a rabbit.

I don't know how many days we rode, and I didn't much care about that. The thing is, we were making good progress. Some days were harder an' hotter than others, but we kept on rolling. When we came upon the wide wooden board nailed to a fence post with HULBERTON hand-lettered on it, we felt like we'd arrived at the promised land.

The sign, like all such signs, was riddled with pistol bullet holes and shot scars.

"We might just as well do it right," I said, and pulled the Sharps out of the sheath that'd once held my 30.30. That rifle was snugged down over my bedroll. I put a round into the sign from about fifty yards out, blowing half of it spinning away, leaving the sign reading HULB.

We rode into town as the sun was beginning its downward journey. The tinkling of the honky-tonk of the piano in a gin mill was the first thing we heard. Hulberton was much the same as all the West Texas towns: four saloons, counting the bar in the restaurant, a church, a rather small mercantile, a cabinet maker and funeral man, a doctor's office, a bank, a whorehouse, and at the end of the main—and only—street, a stable and blacksmith operation. There were a few private homes strewn around the outskirts of the town—shoddy-looking affairs with chickens, pigs, or both wandering around them. The usual town dogs came snarling and snapping at us. Arm gave his horse all his rein so he could drop his head—a horse can't kick out unless he drops his head far down—and the horse nailed what looked to be a critter with more than a little timber wolf blood running through its veins. The dog sailed maybe ten feet in the air before hitting hard and rolling along another few feet. He slunk off into an alley, lips curled back over his fangs, but it was obvious he was finished for the day. The others followed into the alley.

The stable looked like a tight operation. The sale horses were decent, and the corral had two large troughs, both of which were almost full of water. The smith was working at his forge and anvil, turning shoes from bar stock. Blacksmithing isn't a job for a weak man, and this fellow had forearms as big as hams and arm muscles larger yet.

Arm and I swung down and stood back until the smith finished the shoe he was working on and tossed it into a large bucket of water, where it hissed and sizzled for a moment.

I held out my hand. "I'm Jake," I said. "This here's my pard, Armando—Arm, usually." The smith shook with each of us. Grasping his hand was like squeezing a brick. He was tall—taller than me and I'm pushing six feet, and much of his face was hidden by a thick black beard.

"I'm called Tiny," he said, grinning. "As a kid I beat the shit out of anyone who called me Tiny, but they all kept it up—adults, too—an' I got used to it. Anyway, my real handle is Forsythe Dragonovich, so I figure Tiny beats that all to hell." He paused. "What can I do for you boys?"

"How about new shoes all the way around on both of our horses an' a trim on the packer? Maybe put some crimped oats in front of them and kinda look them over—make sure they're in good shape. We've covered some ground lately."

Tiny glanced at our horses. "They don't look the worse for it," he said. "I'll take care of them, get some oats into them."

"Ees good," Arm said. "I'm wonderin'—are you a man who'd maybe drink some beer?"

The blacksmith's grin flashed again. "You can bet your eyes on that, Arm," he said. "You boys stayin' the night?"

"I figured we would—get a decent meal an' some rest," I said.

"Good," Tiny said. "I'll finish up your horses an' be along directly to suck some beer. Go on over to Donovan's"—he pointed at a saloon—"their beer is cold 'nuff to freeze yer nuts off."

"The food at the hotel any good?" I asked.

"Decent. Beats jerky, anyway, an' the plates 're big. Fair to middlin' steaks."

"We'll give it a try later. Right now we're gonna walk on over to Donovan's an' drink beer while we wait on you."

Cold beer is a real luxury and cost another nickel a mug over the warm because the saloon had to cut ice in the winter an' warehouse it under sawdust 'til it's needed. Best nickels I ever spent, to my way of thinking.

Arm strode directly to the bar, tugging a fistful of ones and fives out of his pocket as he did so. I gave him a few steps and moved off to the side a bit, hands at my sides. They're still lots of places in Texas where a man'd rather shoot a Mex than a rattlesnake.

Arm dropped the cash on the bar. "We weel be at a table an' Tiny is joinin' us in a bit. See, we wan' to drink all the cold beer you got. Tell me when we run outta money. We got more."

The bartender laughed. "Hell, with Tiny sittin' in, you might could do that."

We walked to a back table and sat down. There were a dozen or so other men in the bar and a couple of poker games going on. Nobody paid us any attention after a quick, cursory look. In a couple of minutes the bartender came over with six mugs on a tray, set the mugs on the table, said, "Have at it, boys," and went back to the bar with his tray.

We had at it.

The beer was teeth-shattering cold and had the strong, yeasty taste to it that real beer drinkers seek out but don't find too often.

We'd been sitting there drinking for ten minutes or so, yapping about the ranch. For a quick moment, conversation in the saloon stopped—not ours, but everyone else's. I looked up at the man who'd just pushed through the bat wings and was walking over toward us. He was tall, gaunt-looking, and his shirt and pants sagged on him. His Colt was tied to his leg. He was clean shaven although his hair reached his shoulders. He stood at our table.

"My name's Turner," he said. "I work for Mr. Dansworth—he runs this town. I don't suppose you boys would care to give me one of those fine mugs of beer?"

"Help yourself," I said. "Plenty more where that came from."

He did so and took a long, appreciative drink. "Funny thing," he said. "Somebody blew our sign in half earlier. I stopped over to say hello to Tiny and I saw the stock of a Sharps sticking out of a saddle sheath in his shop. Strange coincidence, no?"

"We buy nice new sign," Arm said. "Any price. Don' matter."

"Oh? That's purely kind of you. By the way, you boys have names?"

"I'm Jake—this is Armando. You need last names?"

"No. But you can tell me what you're doing in Hulberton."

"I just inherited a ranch from a fella named Hiram Ven Gelpwell," I said. "I got a document in my shirt pocket. I'll reach in and get it if you want—or you can go after it to make sure I'm not pulling a Derringer on you."

"You get it," Turner said. "If you shot me you'd never get outta here alive."

I retrieved the document and handed it to Turner. He pulled out a chair and sat down to read it. "One beer makes a man thirsty," he commented.

"Like my partner said, there's plenty more where that came from. Help yourself."

Turner drained his first mug and picked up a second and returned to his reading. "Damn," he said, "you got six thousand dollars in this deal, too? Was ol' man Ven Gelpwell in love with you or something?"

"I never met him. He was a friend of my mother's a long time ago."

"Well," Turner said, "all this legal horseshit is in order, far's I can tell. What're you gonna do with the place?"

I launched into my dissertation on how we were going to breed, raise, and train the best working horses in the West.

"You been out to look things over yet?"

"Nope. We figured we'd have a decent meal and a decent sleep 'fore we rode out to it."

"You won't get a whole lot of hay or grain out of it—it's awfully rocky and the good soil is shallow. You might better sharecrop it out an' take your cut in hay an' oats. I know a couple families who'd be right interested."

"Fine. I'd like to talk with them."

Turner nodded. "I'll send them on out in a day or so." He took a long drink. "You got a good number of free-range beef out there—you ain't gonna starve. But you watch yourself and your horse around them. Those goddamn longhorns would just as soon rip a horse's gut as he would graze sweet grass. I was you, I'd pick one off from a good distance off with that Sharps an' then drag him in to butcher."

"We'll keep that in mind," I said.

Turner set down his empty mug and stood. "One more thing. Like I said, Mr. Dansworth runs Hulberton. He's got me an' a good number of others to help him out. He's a horseman—you might both be lookin' for the same thing."

"Lotsa horses aroun'," I said. "Enough for everybody."

"Sure," Turner said. "Long as Mr. Dansworth gets the best there won't be no trouble. But don't ever mess with him. Hear? You'll end up dead, you do."

"Thass a threat?" Arm asked.

"You bet it is. An' it's a bet you boys can't win."

"Boolshit," Arm commented.

"We don't take to threats real well," I said.

Turner's entire demeanor changed from friendly cowhand to dangerous enemy. "Doesn't seem to me either of you is real smart, then. You cause us any grief an' you'll regret it real quick."

Chapter Two

Tiny walked in a few moments after Turner left. The blacksmith nodded at and greeted most of the men in the bar and pulled up a chair at our table. "Damn," he said, "after a day wrestling with horses, a man gets a strong thirst."

Arm waved his arm over the just-replenished mugs on the table like a magician drawing attention to a feat he's just performed.

Tiny drank mugs of beer like other men down shots of whiskey: he picked up the mug, brought it to his mouth, tilted his head back, and swallowed the beverage all in one smooth, well-practiced move. He performed this four times and then waved to the tender for more beer. "Ahhhhh," he sighed happily. "If that don't go down nice, I sure don't know what does."

"Our horses check out good?" I asked.

"Oh, yeah. There were some minor quarter cracks on the Appy, but I took care of them. The packer's okay, 'cept for his age. He's probably older than God. It looks like he still has some years left in him, though."

Tiny told us what he knew about the place I'd inherited. "Ol' Ven Gelpwell 'cropped out most of the land, which ain't a bad idea. You'll need to do some fencing. But hell, the barn an' house are good. I'd say you boys lucked into a real sweet spread."

He downed another beer. "Say—a ranch gotta have a name. Wadda ya gonna call yours?"

I scratched my head. "I haven't given it any thought," I said. "But you're right." I was quiet for a moment. "How about 'Hulberton Fine Working Horses'?"

Armando laughed. "Ees stupid. Me, I like, 'SantaMaria Best Horses.'"

"That's awful, Arm. Why do we need to advertise your family name? An' the 'Best' isn't right, either."

"Bullshit. I theenk . . ."

I waved Arm's next idea away and spoke directly to Tiny. "Did Ven Gelpwell have a root cellar or a place to hang beef? I'm gonna fetch in a head of those free-rangers soon's I can—I favor beef almost as well as I do beer."

"Yeah—he had a little dugout where he stored apples an' potatoes an' salted-down ham. I ain't seen it in a while, but I'd guess it's still there. But lemme ask you this: why not take one of them wild pigs 'stead of a beef? You're gonna lose lots of good meat no matter how careful you are with cattle, but a pig, why hell—you can use everything but the squeal. Beef's cheaper'n penny candy in town. I'd get me a pig, I was you."

Arm and I looked at each other. "Makes sense," I said. Arm nodded. "I put a loop over one of these *porgos* soon as I can. There are many 'round?"

"Yeah. They're tricky little bastards, so watch

yourself. A big stud or even a sow will charge a horse, knock him right off his feet. Sonsabitches are wild but they make pretty good eatin'. Leave the big tuskers alone. They're godawful crazy. Shoot any I see, is what I'd do."

"There ees a stream, no?"

"A damn fine one—a year-'rounder. Rarer than teats on a boot 'round here. Gets awful low this time of year, but she keeps on runnin'."

We drank for another hour or so. Arm and I had the staggers a tad, but Tiny didn't show any effects of the beer.

"I think it's time me an' Arm got us a meal an' a bed," I said.

"Might not be a bad idea for me to head home, too. The ol' lady will start in on me if I stay out too long."

The three of us stood and started toward the bat wings.

"Boys," the tender called. "You got change comin'—a good bit of it."

"Call it a tip an' put it in your pocket," I said. "We'll be seein' you again."

Tiny headed back to the stables and Arm and I weaved our way to the hotel, took a couple of rooms, and went into the six-table restaurant. We both ordered steaks from a cadaverous waiter who probably hadn't smiled during this century. We also ordered more beer.

Tiny had said the plates were big, and he wasn't exaggerating. They looked the size of wagon wheels and still the steaks were too big for the plates and hung off the edges. The meat was a tad tough, but the flavor was great. Neither of us left a scrap of meat on our plates, and had scraped clean the big bowl of mashed potatoes the waiter had brought without being asked.

Arm leaned back in his chair and belched. "I'm ready to meet my bed," he said, and yawned.

"Me, too. Let's do it."

The rooms weren't a whole lot bigger than closets, but the beds had real mattresses rather than shucks and sawdust. I fell onto mine bed fully dressed except for my hat, and I assume Arm did the same with his. I was asleep immediately.

Well before dawn a goddamn rooster right below my window started his racket. I heard a gunshot from the adjacent room. Blessed silence returned and I went back to sleep.

It must have been near seven thirty or eight o'clock when we met up down in the restaurant. I don't think I'd slept that long since I was in a cradle. Both our hangovers were mild and we were both hungry as bears coming out of hibernation. The cadaver hustled over and I ordered six eggs, steaks like we had the night before, and hash-brown potatoes. At first, the ol' fellow thought we were going to split that plate. I made certain he realized we individually wanted what I'd ordered.

We chowed down and drank a pot of coffee. When the waiter brought the bill, I noticed he'd added on fifty-five cents for the rooster Armando gunned. We paid up for the grub, the rooms, and left a good tip.

The day promised to be another that'd almost raise blisters on a man's skin. We walked down to the stable. Tiny's anvil was ringing like a bell in spite of the heat. We gave Tiny a fifty to open an account for us, saddled up our horses, and packed our old fellow. I asked Tiny where our ranch was. "Straight east, maybe four or five miles," he said.

The first sign that told us we were on our land was some broken-down fencing that'd once been a couple-acre corral. "We're home," I said.

"*Sí*," Arm said, "feels right, no?"

"Yeah. It feels right, pard."

We could barely see the top of the barn because of the lay of the land—fairly gentle rises and slopes. We plodded along, sweltering.

"Peeg," Arm whispered. "Over there—in the scrub." He loosened his throwing rope from the latigo strip on his saddle. His black horse, dripping sweat, perked up immediately, Arm transmitting his excitement to the animal. I took a tighter grip on the packer's lead line. Arm shook out a good loop and nudged his horse with his spurless heels. The black took off as if he were fired from a cannon, his hooves flinging clumps of dried buffalo grass and dirt behind him.

The pig—a young one, maybe a hundred, a hundred and fifty pounds—burst out of the scrub and began covering ground in that clumsy-looking but actually quite fast way they have of running.

Arm was up and next to the pig in a few seconds, swinging a loop over his head. The pig wasn't stupid; he cut sharply to his left, putting Arm both behind and way the hell out of position to throw. He caught the pig and the same thing happened. Arm's horse was sucking air but still working hard. This time, when they got close enough to throw at, the pig cut to the right—a move Arm and his horse were expecting. Arm's loop struck out like a striking snake and dropped over the pig's head. At that very moment, Arm's horse stumbled, banging a front hoof against a rock. Arm screamed, shaking his right hand as he snubbed the rope over his saddle horn. Somehow, he'd gotten his thumb in a small coil of the close end of the rope as he did so. I could hear the thumb snap from twenty yards away.

The pig hit the end of the rope and flipped up, crashing down on his back, squealing. "Sonommabeetch!" Armando shouted, and made a cross-draw with his left hand to the pistol on his right leg and put six rounds into the pig. "*Jesús Cristo,* that hurts," he said.

"Why the hell didn't you just take the pig out with the Sharps?" I asked.

"Ees bad luck. A man captures his first food on his land. Thass the way it's always been." He held his left hand out in front of him. The thumb was already twice its normal size and the nail was mostly gone.

"And this is good luck?" I asked.

He glared at me for a long moment, his eyes burning like embers. "The name of theese ranch is now an' forever 'The Busted Thumb Horse Ranch.' *Sí?*"

Arguing at that point would have been stupid and maybe dangerous. Anyway, I figured it was a name folks wouldn't forget. "Agreed, Armando," I said. "Now, let's get a splint on that thumb an' wrap it good. I'll drag the pig on to the house."

"I need the liquor first to dull the pain."

" 'Course you do." I fetched an unopened quart from the packhorse and brought it to Arm, who'd swung down from his horse. While he sucked at the booze I looked around for a good, straight stick in the brush. I went back to the packhorse, dug out my winter long johns, and tore off a sleeve, which I then cut in strips with my boot knife.

Arm was pale faced but ready for me.

"No other way to do this, partner," I said.

"Do eet. The longer you talk the bigger the goddamn thumb gets."

Armando clamped his teeth together as I set the splint and took a dozen or more wraps around it with the long john fabric. Only occasionally did a moan escape him. When I was finished he further anesthetized himself with booze. "You done it good, Jake," he said. "Still hurt some, though."

Arm climbed onto his horse. I walked out to the end of the rope and took a wrap around my saddle horn. We rode toward the barn and house, the pig bouncing on and over the uneven, rocky land. The packhorse, scared but not scared enough to bolt, came along docilely, although his ears were back and his eyes wide.

The house was a pretty old thing and looked to be in decent repair. What surprised me was the hugely fat lady on the porch, sweeping furiously, almost enveloping herself in a cloud of grit. From inside we could hear an off-key song bellowed out in Spanish. There was a small two-horse farm wagon tied to the hitching rail in the shade of the barn.

I know a few words of Spanish: *puta, pendejo,* and the like, but that's about it. Arm obviously had no such problem and lit into a conversation with the sweeper. They went back and forth quickly, Arm grinning in spite of his thumb, the lady answering two- or three-word questions with long and dramatic-sounding paragraphs.

"Tiny," Arm said to me, "sent these two fine ladies out to clean the house for us. This *mamacita* is Blanca and the one singing inside is Teresa. We're supposed to pay them a buck or two."

Blanca hefted herself down the two stairs from the porch to the ground and followed the rope to where it was around the pig's neck. She said something to Arm.

"Blanca and her pard weel butcher an' salt the pig for a dollar."

"I ain't much of a butcher," I said. "Tell them to do it. Let's go inside an' give the house a look-see."

Teresa was the exact opposite of Blanca; she was as thin as a stalk of green wheat. She was flailing a feather duster around. She smiled at us but kept her singing going.

There wasn't a whole lot of furniture in the living room: a horsehair-covered couch, a pair of big, soft chairs, a small table, and three lanterns hanging from the walls. The floor was hardwood and it gleamed—the ladies must have scrubbed hell out of it. There was a good-size fireplace; a Confederate officer's hat and a saber were mounted above the mantelpiece.

We wandered into the kitchen. There was an inside pump, a sink, and a bunch of cupboards. I pulled one open. It was filled with precisely aligned bottles of tequila. There must have been a dozen of them. The rest of the cupboards were empty except for mouse shit and spiderwebs.

Arm grabbed a bottle, pulled the cork with his teeth, and drank. "Mediceen," he said after a moment. "Good for thumbs."

There were two bedrooms upstairs and a small room that could have been an office or even a kid's room, although nobody had mentioned if Ven Gelpwell had been married or had a child with him. The ladies must have gotten out here in the dark: the upstairs was clean and smelled of furniture polish. There were mattresses on the beds, both of which were piss stained. We'd slept in worse places.

We meandered out to the barn. I've always respected a tight, well-built barn, and this one was as good as they came. The big front doors swung easily, although they needed a bit of oil on their hinges. The stalls—eight of them—were 12'×12', which is a good size. There was a birthing stall, too. The ladder to the hay storage above was stout and sturdy and the floor up there was plenty strong enough to support all the hay we could cram into it.

When we came back down a five-foot rattler was sliding out of one of the stalls. Arm drew and killed the snake. "We can't have no rattlers 'round," he said, "but I weel bet we got no mice or rats. We leave blacksnakes alone, no?"

I could see that Armando's thumb still hurt pretty bad, in spite of the tequila. His face was pale, too. "If you tell the ladies to get to the pig, we can cook up a batch of pork chops, Arm. 'Til they're ready, you can get some rest."

"I don' need no res'," he said, but it was a matter of form for him. Revealing any weakness of any kind would make him, in his mind, less of a man. He went to the porch and spoke with Blanca, and then waved me over.

"The ladies weel do the pig now an' then continue with the cleaning of the house. I weel try a bed to see does it make for sleep."

I dragged the pig over to a tall tree between the house and barn that I'd noticed had butchering arms screwed into a large branch. I removed the throwing rope from the pig as the women approached with a pair of medium-weight chains from the barn. They cut into the pig's hocks, inserted a pair of hooks, and hefted the animal up as if it were a kitten. There was a cauldron off to the side with a pit under it for a fire. There was a good stock of wood already in it. Blanco struck a match to some kindling and got the fire going at several points. When Teresa stuck a fourteen-inch blade into the pig's anus and cut upward, I turned away and went back into the barn. I'd seen butchering before, but that didn't mean I enjoyed watchin' it. I heard the guts dump out of the animal and strike the ground, and it made me shudder.

I stood in the barn, listening to the minor creaks and groans that are always present in such a massive wooden structure. I looked around again, and shook my head in disbelief.

We've got everything we need now—land, house, barn, and money. There's stock around. Tiny will know who owns what we might need and we'd crossed mustang herd tracks several times as we rode from Hulberton. It wasn't going to be easy to find the right horses, because temperament was just as important as physical traits. A horse that's lazy, or fights his owner, or fights too often with the other horses would be no good to us. Both my horse and Arm's were geldings— and they didn't quite make the grade of what we wanted as breeding stock, even if they'd been stallions.

Mustangs tend to be a bit nutsy because they've been free for so many generations, and they were all rope-shy and distrustful. Sometimes a mustang can be brought down and made into a useful horse, but there was always the chance he'd revert to type and pull some kind of a stunt like rolling on his rider. Still, generalizations never apply to all of anything, be it horses, dogs, or people. All I knew was that it was going to take some looking to find what we were after, but both Armando and I were dead-on convinced that the horses we needed existed.

That evening Arm wasn't at all interested in a plate of pork chops—one of his favorite feeds. His thumb looked bad—hugely swollen and skintight with that shiny red of illness. His only interest was another jug of tequila and his bed. Blanca and Teresa checked him out and both shook their heads in dismay. Teresa rattled off some Spanish to Arm. He answered in English: "I don't have no goddamn infection."

The ladies were back before full light the next morning. Arm was both listless and surly, if those two attributes can both function at the same time, which they apparently can. I sat with him as the sun rose.

"Look," I said, "you do what Blanca and Teresa tell you without handing them a ton of shit. I'm going out with the glasses to take a peek at whatever mustangs I cross. If your thumb isn't better by the time I get back, we'll have to find a doctor somehow."

"Doctors, they are boolshit," he said. "Busted thumbs don' need no doctors." His eyes were closing. I let him drift back to sleep and then left.

We'd won a pair of U.S. military binoculars in a poker game in Yuma a couple of years back. We were careful of them and rarely used them. I took them tucked in their case along with me.

The temperature wasn't real bad and my horse was frisky. I let him sunfish a bit when I settled in the saddle and ran him for a mile or so until he clamed down. It gave me a strange feeling to realize that I was riding on land my partner and me owned.

I crossed a herd's tracks within a couple of hours and followed them easily. It was beyond midday when I topped a little ridge and saw the herd—maybe forty head—clustered around a small water hole. Most were mares. The honcho stallion was a roan, and he stood off from the rest, muzzle high, testing the breeze. The breeze was coming from them to me, which stopped the stud from catching my scent. I looked him over through the glasses. He wasn't much of a horse. His front end had no chest to speak of; it looked like his forelegs came out of the same hole. His legs were almost ruler straight with no angle to the pasterns. His spine sagged, and his ass, although large and powerful-looking, wouldn't do anything for him because I doubted that he had any wind, given the scrawniness of his chest. I figured it wouldn't be too long before some young stud kicked holes in him and took over the herd.

There were a couple decent-looking mares at the water, but nothing the Busted Thumb would have any interest in.

I rode back to the ranch, a bit disappointed. I'm not real sure of what I was expecting from the mustangs, but whatever it was, I didn't get it.

I put my horse in his stall with fresh water and walked into the house and up to Armando's room. The ladies had taken the wrapping off his thumb and had his arm extended out to the side. The thumb was huge, grotesque-looking, and little trails of red were running from it down his forearm. "Infection?" I asked.

"*Sí*," Teresa answered. "*Mal infección.*"

The room reeked of tequila and Arm was passed out. Blanca was sharpening a short knife on a stone, dipping it into a glass of tequila every so often. Teresa told me—through hand motions and by grasping my arm—what she and Blanca wanted me to do: hold Armando's arm extended out while Blanca drained the infection and poured in a brownish liquid from a large vial she had wrapped in a thick wool cloth.

I did as I was told. I held my partner's arm out—keeping my hands as far away from his thumb as I could.

Blanca stood over Arm. His thumb was up and pointing at her, and the little red trails seemed to have gotten larger. I noticed, too, that there was a musty scent of sweetish rot around Arm's hand.

Blanca was handy with her knife. She cut a slash the length of Arm's thumb. I gagged as greenish pus spurted several inches into the air, following her blade. She let the wound bleed for several minutes and then carefully uncorked her vial. Her eyes met mine and the message was clear: *hold on.* She poured the brownish liquid into the cut. Armando was instantly awake and screaming in pain. Teresa, sitting on his right arm, was bounced about like a bronc man on a rank horse.

Blanca waited for a few moments and poured a second time. Armando began another scream— and then passed out. I thought he was dead.

Teresa climbed off his arm and helped Blanca resplint and rewrap the thumb. Then both women stood back from the bed. *"Muy bueno,"* Blanca said. Teresa smiled.

It took me a moment to see that Arm's chest was moving normally as he breathed, and that he seemed in no discomfort. I damned near ran down the stairs to the kitchen and the cupboard with the tequila in it. Then, I got drunk. But before I did I handed each woman a fifty-dollar bill when they came downstairs. Their eyes widened: fifty bucks was a ton of money to them. The surprise on their faces faded, to be replaced with wide, happy smiles.

They left in their farm wagon shortly afterward.

Not having Arm to talk to and drink with felt strange. I sat out on the porch until dark and then went inside, lit a lantern, and sat in one of the big chairs and stared at the wall.

Rain is as rare as an honest riverboat gambler in West Texas. Sometime during the night after Blanca and Teresa treated Arm, however, a light rain began—and kept on falling for the next three days.

In a sense, it was a gift to Armando: during that time he alternated between sleeping, watching rain snakes course down the windowpanes, and drinking tequila. He seemed content enough during his rain-enforced recuperation.

I, on the other hand, was going crazy. I had nothing to do, no one to talk to, and was sick of eating pork chops. Midday of the second day I saddled my horse, pulled on my slicker, and rode to Hulberton, tense all the way because I could feel my horse's hooves sliding when they should have purchasing traction. I made it there, though.

I found Tiny sitting on a bale of straw. There was no fire in his forge. Only two of his stalls had horses in them, and his for-sale horses were clustered under an A-frame shelter he'd built in his corral.

His face lit up when I rode in—as mine did when I saw him. "Pull up a bale," he said, "an' we can both be bored to death together," he said. "How's Arm's paw?"

"Real good. Blanca and Teresa fixed him up jus' fine. Those are great ladies, Tiny."

"Sure 'nuff. But I gotta show you somethin' they done for you boys. Damn, Jake, them fifties were more'n their families had saw in their best year."

We went to the rear of his barn. Leaning against his baled hay was a fourteen-foot, twelve-inch board of wood painted a pure white. On it were the precisely painted words, THE BUSTED THUMB HORSE RANCH.

"We had to go to the sherrif," Tiny said, "to do the spelling right. I ain't much at it. Pretty sign, ain't it? All you boys gotta do is get uprights an' nail her up."

I ran my hand along the sign. "Damn," I said, "they sanded this plank. It's as smooth as a baby's ass."

"Yep. They spent some time an' some muscle on it, Jake."

I didn't know what to say. "I don't know no Spanish, but I'll make sure Arm thanks the ladies proper. That sign's beautiful."

We went back up to the front of the barn. "You ain't got much hay," Tiny said. "And what I seen there was cactus spines an' prairie dog shit. I just got a load of green trefoil mix in. I can let it go for twelve cents a tight bale."

"I'll tell you what, Tiny—you haul the shit outta our barn an' sell us a thousand bales at your price. Can you do it?"

"Sure."

"Okay. Now, we got some crimped oats but it's all piss-poor. You want to empty our bins an' re-fill 'em with your feed?"

"Well, sure."

"How about a heavy mix of molasses in the grain? Can you do that?"

Tiny chuckled. "Can I make my ol' lady scratch my back an' call, 'Oh God, oh God?' I can mix grain an' molasses, Jake—don't you worry none about that."

"Good."

Tiny looked embarrassed. " 'Course, we're talk-ing about some money here. The hay—an' that fancied-up grain, an' the delivery—will run maybe . . ."

I held up my hand. "I don't give a damn. Tell me what you need an' I'll give it to you right now."

"On delivery is good," Tiny said. "Includin', 'course, a taste of ol' man Ven Gelpwell's tequila."

We sat on our bales for another minute or so. One of the horses in a stall whinnied for what-ever reason.

"That fella's catchin' the scent of mare out there who's lookin' for a stud," Tiny said. "I ain't gonna breed him. He's a nice enough horse, but he's as clumsy as a drunk an' got no speed, either. Good temperament, but hell—that ain't gonna take him too far."

"No. I s'pose not. Me an' Arm are lookin' for fine brood mares an' a stud horse that's . . . well . . . he's gotta be the best."

Tiny nodded. "Look," he said. "I don't know if this is any good, but I had an Apache in here yes-tiddy for me to fix up a bad hoof crack on his pony. He said he seen a big mustang herd—maybe a hundred head or so—with a stud run-nin' the show. He said the stallion was the fantasmo horse."

"Fantasmo?"

"Yeah—as good as they get: faster, stronger, all that. Can't be killed or captured."

"Where was this herd?"

"Up near the foothills—maybe thirty miles, kinda south-southeast."

"You know this Apache fella?"

"No—I never seen him before."

"You get his name?"

"He Who Walks Far. Thing is, he's a hostile. Busted the reservation, shot up some soldiers, took a few scalps, wrecked a couple white girls."

"Well," I said, "me an Arm want to see this stud horse—if he's real. We don't give a damn 'bout the hostile. This Apache who done the little girls don't deserve life, and we'd just as soon put a bullet in him, an' maybe we will some day. But, what we're lookin' for is horses."

"Well, according to this Apache, he's supposed to be a big, tall bay. He said this fantasmo's eyes glow like fire in the night an' his hooves strike sparks when he runs." Tiny sighed. "I wouldn't get too excited, though—the Indian mighta been eatin' them mushroom buds that make them see things, or maybe he jus' dreamed all that stuff. Every so often there's a rumor 'bout a fantasmo horse, but it never amounts to nothin'. Still, I hear talk every now an' again."

"What about the herd, though? You think that's real?"

"Yeah. Fact is, I *know* it is, 'cause I seen them maybe a year ago. Me an' my brother-in-law was out hunting and we seen tracks, first. Then, later, we seen the herd. They were far off an' there was lots of dust 'round them an' we couldn't see no tall bay, but I'll tell you this, Jake: we seen a hundred or more mustangs. They was out south an' east, maybe twenty or twenty-five miles from town. That don't mean nothin', though. You know how them mustangs range."

We sat there for a while, watching the rain. "What about our packer, Tiny?" I asked. "If me an' Arm set out, can that boy take it?"

Tiny plucked a length of straw out of the bale he was sitting on and stuck it in the corner of his mouth. He chewed a bit before he spoke. "That ol' packer looks like he was put together outta clay twigs. But—an' here's the thing—have you ever took a good look at the way he's put together?"

"Well, we were in a hurry an' Arm—"

"Hush now an' listen, okay?"

I nodded.

"As a ridin' horse, you might better buy a goat or some such. But as a pack animal, that boy is damned near perfect. He's put together jus' right to carry weight. He ain't got a clumsy bone in his body—the sumbitch could probably walk a tightrope in a hurricane an' not miss a step. He's good—an' you ain't gonna do no better. Hear?"

"Yeah—I hear. Like I said, I didn't pick him out—Arm did. So I can't take no credit. But when Arm's busted thumb is healed enough to travel, we're gonna go an' see if we can't find that herd—an' maybe that fantasmo."

"Don't count on no fantasmo. But you'll find the herd, do you look hard enough. There could might be a mare or two that you want."

I'd put $500 together to give to Tiny. "Me an' Arm, we gotta ask a favor of you. Here's five hundred dollars. If you come across or see a stud you think is worth the money, you hand it on over. If the horse ain't what me an' Arm need, you keep the horse an' you don't owe us nothin'—an if there's money left over, it's yours. 'Course if you wanted to set the three of us up for a night of cold beer, why hell, that'd work."

Tiny laughed. "I can do that. I can't promise I'll find the horse you boys are looking for, but I'll do my best."

"Good. That's all we want."

Tiny stood from his bale. "I think we oughta try that beer right now—make sure it's jus' right."

It sounded good, but I turned down Tiny's offer. "I gotta get back, see if Arm is lookin' good. I don't like ridin' in rain, but a man can't always get what he wants."

On the ride back I saw that the rain was tapering off. The day was bleak and the sky was a thick blanket of gray, but the air smelled fresher and less like the reek of constant rain.

Armando was downstairs, stretched out on the couch. "You know," he said in lieu of a greeting, "we got no food 'cept pork. I'm damned near starved to death."

"Yeah. I know. I should have loaded up while I was in town, but didn't think of it. The rain's about stopped, though."

Armando grumbled something I didn't quite catch.

"I spent some time with Tiny," I said. "You ever hear of a fantasmo horse?"

"Boolshit. Is kid's talk. But sure, I've heard."

"Probably. But Tiny told me there's a herd of about a hundred's tangs out there, an' that he'll keep his eyes an' ears open for the both brood mares an' studs for us."

"Ees. Good. Ya know, it might take us a long

time to get the Busted Thumb up an' running, no?"

"Maybe."

Arm straightened on the couch and got to his feet. He attempted a step and then fell back on his ass on the couch. "Dizzy," he said. "I need maybe *una mas* day an' then we go out after that herd, no?"

"I guess that depends on whether or not you can sit your horse without falling off. Tomorrow I'll take our packer in an' load up on grub. Maybe the day after we can go out."

Arm swung his legs back up on the couch and stretched out again. "*Sí*," he said.

The next morning brought one of those blessed dry days with sun, blue sky, and not an awful lot of heat. Arm was sleeping when I went out to the barn and I left him alone. I strapped on the packer's rig, saddled my horse, and rode to town. I picked up what I needed at the mercantile quickly, bought an extra sack of coffee and some tobacco and rolling papers, and wandered over to Tiny's. He didn't have much business; he was sitting on a bale of hay looking off at nothing I could see.

"Looks like Arm and me are goin' out to see about that herd with the fantasmo horse," I said.

"Figured you would. Thing is, from what I heard, you'll have to kill him to bring him in. He's a rank one, Jake."

"I've handled rank ones before," I said. "Hell, when I was breakin' horses I rode some that came straight from hell."

Tiny nodded but didn't speak.

"Anyway," I said, "I guess we'll see."

"Yep. How long you figure to be out?"

"I dunno. Until we find the herd an' get a look at this stud, I guess."

"Might take a while. I'll keep a watch over your place while you're gone."

" 'Preciate it, Tiny."

There didn't seem to be much of anything else to say, so I mounted up, took the packer's lead rope, waved to Tiny, and rode on home to the ranch.

Arm was as feisty as a bucket of scorpions a couple days later when we figured he could travel all right. He always got this way for some reason when we were setting out on something big—and he was just as friendly as a mountain cat with a white-hot poker up its ass. He'd been out in the barn before light, working under the flickering light of ol' man Ven Gelpwell's 'Sure Star' lanterns.

" 'Bout goddamn time," he growled as I walked into the barn, building a smoke.

"Mornin' to you, too, Arm."

"You figure that packer's gonna toss his rig on all by hisself?" Arm snarled.

I saddled my horse first, just to put another prickly pear under Arm. When he heard the glug and tinkle of a couple of bottles in my saddlebag, his face grew red with anger."

"*Madre de Jesús*, this ain't no barroom drinkin' party, Jake. We go to fetch horses, no? An' maybe a fantasmo horse what probably don't even exist, case you forgot."

I ignored Arm and we finished our preparations. I checked all twelve shoes for tightness. "Ready?" I asked.

Armando smiled for the first time that day. "Ready," he said.

We rode in a roughly south-southeast direction. It was scarcely full light and the scents and sensations of the virgin dew sweet in the air made a man feel fresh and good. Our horses' shoes clinked every so often on a rock, seeming to ring like a bell that'd carry all 'cross Texas.

The day heated up, but without the life-sapping fire of full summer. We were at the end of August according to the calendar in the mercantile, and the weather 'round here changed real quickly. September snow an' ice storms weren't terribly rare.

We camped early but neither of us was awful hungry. Thing is, we hit a little spring-fed watering hole an' just couldn't pass it and the few desert pines up. We ate jerky and drank coffee. About dark, Arm cleared his throat. "Uhh . . . that booze you brought along . . ."

I fetched the bottle and we each had a couple snorts.

"We will hit tracks maybe two days, maybe more," Armando said. "A big herd like you say, even a *Anglo* could follow."

I let that pass.

Mustangs tend to cover a lot of ground in their daily search for grass and water, but they tend to stay in pretty much the same areas. If we rode long enough, it was a pretty sure thing we'd come upon the horses or their tracks, and Arm and I both knew that, so there was no real hurry.

Arm's horse picked up a shard of rock between his shoe and hoof in his left front and by midday began favoring it. I dug it out with my Barlow knife and we packed it with mud and the horse grunted in the way of thanks. We made camp right there to make sure the hoof was okay.

I walked out to scrounge up a meal. Armando won't eat snake—some Mexican mumbo jumbo forbids it—and I passed by a couple of fat rattlers taking the sun on rocks. They'd have made a good stew and broiling pieces on sticks over a fire wouldn't have been a bad meal, either.

There were plenty of jackrabbits around and I bagged a pair of fine ones, one shot apiece from a draw, which ain't bad shootin', if I do say so myself.

Arm had a fire going by the time I got back to our camp and I could smell the mesquite burning from a good distance off. One of the few benefits of being an aimless drifter or a cowpoke is that smell—it's fresh and almost sweet and jacks up a man's spirits every time.

We cooked the jacks about dusk and then settled back with a sip of booze, contented, full of stomach, enjoying the sunset.

"Soon, I theenk, we will come on them horses," Arm said.

"We haven't seen a single track or a solitary lump of horse apple, Arm. Could be a while yet."

"Some theengs I jus' know," he said, ending that conversation. Arguing with Armando makes as much sense as arguing with a chicken.

"I'm wonderin' how many we can drive," I said. "They're bound to be as wild as hawks—

even the mares—an' might not take to bein' pushed in one direction."

"We take the stud, his ladies'll follow," Arm said. A rope on either side an' he got no choice, Jake—the sumbitch'll either come or we'll drag him along, no?"

"We'll see, I guess."

In the morning Arm's horse was as fit as a four-month old colt. We lit out early.

We saw no tracks that day and the sun was flexing its end-of-summer muscles. We emptied our canteens into our hats for our horses early on. We hit some piss-poor water late in the day, but it was better than nothing, an' was safe to drink—the tracks around the stingy little puddle proved that. No prairie or desert critter is going to drink water that'll croak him. Somehow, they know what's okay an' what isn't.

Jerky and foul water doesn't make much of a meal, but we ate it anyway, figuring on taking another couple of jacks or prairie hens toward the end of the day.

It was too damned hot to ask our animals for any speed, so we plodded along, dripping sweat.

"Prolly last day of the year we sweat," Arm said. " 'Fore long, we be freezin' our asses off. Makes a man wonder why anyone, they'd decide to live out here," Arm said.

"Well, hell. Free grazin', for one thing. Some of the valleys are the prettiest places on earth, an' the soil ain't ever been turned. It'll grow any-thing. Plus," I added, "it ain't all jammed up with people like bankers an' lawmen an' churches an' such."

"Ees true. Hard men roamin' about though, no? The crazies from after the war, them ones who hangs *los negros,* Quantrill an' his gang, all them're thicker'n fleas on a dog's ass."

"Maybe so. Sure, they're out an' around. But we ain't seen much of them, an' we're tougher than they are. They hate Mexes, too—an' how many you think it'd take to kill you, Arm?"

"Me? Sheet. One crazy maybe half a mile off with one of them Sharps, is all," he answered cryptically.

We'd had enough by late afternoon. We came on a small oasis an' hauled in for the night. There was some scruffy buffalo grass for the horses to gnaw at and a few desert pines and a rocky little pool maybe a couple of feet across and about that in depth of the sweetest water God ever made.

As we were settling in and gathering up some firewood, Armando pointed to the east. "Look," he said.

I looked. There was a stringy, barely discernable line in the sky way beyond us.

"The herd," I said. "It's gotta be the herd."

Chapter Three

There was no reason to hustle. Those horses weren't going anywhere we couldn't find or track them. It was possible, too, that the grit we saw raised was put in the air by another group of roaming mustangs—not the ones we were after. Nevertheless, we were like a pair of kids on the night before Christmas. It didn't hurt that Arm had shot three prairie hens while he was gathering firewood, and they were all cleaned up and ready to be skewered on sticks over the fire.

Our final bottle of whiskey took a significant hit that night.

Neither of us mentioned that we may be chasing something that doesn't exist—this fantasmo stallion—although that cruel little thought was tucked away in the backs of our minds. We'd know what was what as soon as we saw the herd, so there was no sense in worrying over it.

Our packer was loaded and we were in our saddles a tad before first light. The false dawn—that line of soft, almost pastel light that sneaks up over the horizon before the sun makes its appearance was enough for us to see by. Hell, either of us could saddle up in full dark if it was necessary and, in fact, we'd done so more than a couple of times.

The skimpy cloud in the sky told us the herd was still headed mostly east.

"Mus' be valleys that way," Arm said. "Them horses are already thinkin' of winter, no?"

"Must be," I agreed.

The day was a decent one for riding—hot but not stifling. We'd let our animals drink their fill and we topped off our canteens. Other than the water we carried, we were going to have to count on the mustangs to lead us to water during the day. If they went thirsty, so did we.

It's difficult to gauge distance out there; the only landmarks we had were foothills that seemed way the hell ahead of us—maybe forty or fifty miles—so we did the only thing we could, which was to follow the brownish cloud raised by the herd.

About noon we rested our horses and gnawed at jerky, which had all the flavor of dogwood.

It was almost nightfall when we began seeing relatively fresh piles of droppings from the herd. "*Bueno.* We come closer," Arm said, grinning. "Tomorrow we see them."

We saw them the next afternoon.

There was a shallow valley with a ribbon of water snaking through it, and some sparse grass that was a whole lot better than nothing to a mustang herd. We were at the lip, maybe a hundred yards away. We dismounted and ground-tied our horses behind us a good bit to make us less visible. We had a perfect vantage point for observing the herd.

There were seventy-five or so mares, a bunch of which had foals at their sides. The entire herd was scrawny compared to how guys like me an' Arm like to see horses. Many—most—were ribby, and many of the mares showed painful-looking reddish places about the size of a fist at the base of their tails, meaning they had parasites and that they'd rubbed their asses against trees or boulders or whatever they came across to alleviate the itching. The breeze was from them to us, which was greatly to our advantage.

The stallion was something else again. It's probably fair to say that every saddlebum and cowhand knows a good horse when he sees one—just as my partner and I do. This horse was a rare one, a full sixteen hands tall and maybe a hair more, and his muscles were perfectly defined. His chest was wide and powerful. His head was classic, ears fairly small, muzzle as straight as the barrel of a .45, and his eyes placed perfectly. He was a blood bay and his coat looked like polished copper when the sun hit it right.

He was in motion all the time, his muzzle testing the air, his eyes never still, sweeping over his harem and offspring, moving his body to get a better view of whatever he was looking at.

That was the strange thing both Arm and I picked up on. The stallion seemed to shift his hind end to change positions rather than take the easy step with his front feet that would bring him around.

"He has injured leg," Armando said. "Maybe bad hoof—maybe the bone, she is busted."

"Still, he looks real good. If he ain't purely

crazy, he could maybe make a good stud horse for us," I said. "Injuries don't make any difference 'less he'd been born with them an' passed them on to his get."

"Ees true." Arm waited a long moment. "Now what?"

"Hell, I dunno. This little valley isn't a bad place to try to get ropes on the stud, but then we're buying a pig in a poke. I think we should watch a couple three-three days, see how that boy handles himself."

"What peeg? Ees no *gordo*. You talk funny sometimes, Jake."

I sighed. "Forget it, okay? It's jus' something Americans say."

"But, I . . ."

I sighed again. "Let it go for God's sake," I said, speaking louder than I should have.

Arm grumbled something but shut up. We hunkered down and watched the herd drink and crop grass. Arm nudged me and pointed. A young stud—he looked like a two-year-old—stood off to the side of the mares, posturing, snorting, dropping his head and kicking out with his heels. The mares pretty much ignored him, although several heads turned toward his "tough guy" act.

The young stallion was a good-looking horse. He stood fifteen hands or so, was nicely muscled, and moved well. His coat was called "sooty," a color that isn't seen often in mustangs—or other horses, for that matter. What it amounts to is a kind of layer of black, dullish hairs over a deeper, darker black.

As I said, the mares weren't paying him much

attention, but the blood-bay stallion was watching him closely.

Armando chuckled. "That youngster, his blood runs hot. He wishes to take some brides, no?"

"Or some *putas*—I don't think it matters to him."

Sooty worked his way around the group of mares toward the bay, showing off like a schoolboy in front of the girls all the way. The bay turned to face him and snorted, the sound loud and sharp and angry.

When Sooty was fifty feet from the leader of the herd he stopped his shenanigans and stood square, glaring at the bay. Other than a slight digging motion of his right forefoot, he was statue still. The bay took a step toward the youngster and as he did so his left shoulder dropped farther than it should have—whatever injury he had was in his left front leg or hoof.

Sooty, impetuous like all youth, charged, running full out, head extended, teeth exposed, his hooves raising little explosions of dust. The bay rose to meet him, shifted his bulk slightly to the side, and tore a dinner-plate size of hide and hair off his challenger, leaving a raw, bleeding patch on Sooty's side, just behind his withers.

Sooty squealed in pain but whirled about to attack again—with essentially the same result. This time he ignored the pain and reared, striking out at the bay with front hooves that were faster than a rattler's assault—and more deadly. A well-directed hoof could crush the forehead of another horse like an overripe melon.

The bay reared and that's when Armando and

I got a clear view of the horse's left front hoof: it was twisted grotesquely inwardly, making a forty-five-degree angle with his leg. He struck with his right hoof, catching Sooty in the throat, and knocking him off his feet.

That was the bay's strategy, and it worked well. As the younger horse floundered to get to his feet the bay closed his teeth around his right rear leg, just below the hock. We could see the muscles in the bay's neck tighten, become thick strands of steel. Froth dripped from his jaws and he made a slight back-and-forth sawing movement with his entire head.

Sooty flailed his other legs and reached back, mouth gaping, to tear into the bay's neck and throat. He had little strength; the pain from his captured leg all but incapacitated him.

There was a loud snap and Sooty screeched in pain. The lower leg had been almost severed; it was attached only by stands of muscle and flesh. Whitish red, jagged ends of bone appeared but were obscured in seconds by gushets of blood. It poured onto the sandy soil like water from a good well, at first soaking in and then forming a large puddle that grew as we watched it. The young stud's squeals of pain became less strident, fading to what wasn't far from the moan of a seriously injured human. Then, the horse was quiet. A shudder ran through his entire body and that was it. He'd never again challenge another horse.

The scent of the blood frightened the mares. They huddled closer together, eyes wide, their sides touching those of the others, bodies shivering as if with cold.

The bay stood back and watched his opponent bleed out. It didn't take long. Then he turned away and hobbled back to his lookout spot. His gait was strange but not necessarily clumsy; I figured he'd been born with that twisted foot and had become acclimated to it. There'd never be any speed to him, but the size of his harem indicated he was tough and smart.

"That stallion," Arm said admiringly, "he is one hard sonofabitch."

"Yeah. He is. Getting him back to the ranch won't be easy. I don't think there's but one way, Arm. We ride on opposite sides and get loops over his neck. When he tries to attack one of us the other drags him off and the same thing works from both sides. You saw what those jaws can do. If he gets close enough to either of us to get a hold on us or our horses, we'll end up like that sooty over there drawing flies."

"*Es verdad.* But we ride good, stout horses and we done this before." He paused. "I jus' wonder what we'll do with him when we get him home—he ain't gonna like the ranch."

"All we gotta do is get him into the corral with the snubbing post, tie him good, and feed and water him for a few days without pesterin' him. Then, I'll see what I can do to get some manners into him."

"Even after your work he'll always be dangerous, Jake."

"No doubt about it. No bronc man in the world can take a five- or six-year-old like him an' make a cart pony outta him."

"The mares, they will follow."

"Yeah. We'll put them into the north pasture, out of the stallion's sight. There's better grazing there than they're used to, and good water. We'll jus' let 'em get fat while we work with their boss."

"You gon' ride him?"

"I'll get him to accept a blanket an' saddle an' a bit in his mouth, but riding him seems like it'd bust down that tanglefoot even worse."

Armando nodded. "After we get him bred to some good mares, it'll be a long 'leven months to see what comes from the womb. We ain't good at waitin', Jake."

"Yeah. But no horse ranch can run with one stud. We gotta buy or find another two or so after the one we calm is safe to leave alone."

We watched the herd for the rest of the day. They moved about in the dish of land, avoiding Sooty's corpse but otherwise paying it no attention. Yearlings ran and played, striking at enemies only they could see, snorting, ramming around for the sheer hell of it. It was good to watch—Arm and I both reveled in it, watching these big creatures wild and free in nature.

The bay stallion took his position, dropping his head every so often to graze or drink, but as vigilant as an eagle seeking prey.

"A drink would be nice, no?" Arm said.

"It just so happens," I said, "I was thinking the same thing. An' I can fix us up in short order." I walked back down the rise to our horses. I had a metal flask I'd picked up in the mercantile tucked in among my winter long johns an' extra socks. It didn't hold much more than a pint, but it was better'n nothing."

We spent the balance of the day sipping and watching the horses. We made camp shortly before dark, but didn't dare to start a fire. A horse's vision is none too good, his sense of smell is excellent, and smoke would drive them off. We ate jerky and each had a can of peaches and turned in. Sleep came quickly and easily to me. The more I saw that blood bay in my mind, the better he looked.

The herd had moved down the valley during the night, which we'd pretty much expected them to do. They'd cleared the buffalo grass, grazing it to the dirt, and had to continue on to find food.

We left our packer on a long rope tied off to a rock where the mustangs had been the day before. He could scruff at what was left of the grass and he could reach the water. Then, we lit out after the herd.

We didn't attempt to be quiet about it. That stud would hear and smell us pretty much no matter what we did, since the breeze was now blowing from our backs. After a half day we came upon them. The stud was keeping the mares in a tighter group and he nipped at the colts that decided they'd rather play than jog along at mama's side. Each youngster who bought himself a nip shrieked in pain and got back to the herd in a hurry. The boss hoss was out ahead a short distance in front of the mares, sweeping back and forth, stopping only to stick his muzzle into the air to see what news the wind would bring.

"Lookit the set of his ears," Arm said. "He's good an' mad. He don' like this bein' chased shit."

"I noticed. He's gonna be hard to take."

"We'd bes' pick up sticks or something to whack the sumbitch when he comes chargin'. Shaking reins at him won't make no difference."

"Sticks probably won't, either, but you're right. Damn. We shoulda brought heavy quirts. A good cut across the nostrils will stop any horse."

"Mos' horses," Armando corrected.

We followed behind the herd for a couple of hours. They weren't moving fast but they were moving steadily. The stud let them stop at a water hole and drink, but shagged them out a few minutes later. There were a couple of young desert pines near the water; we each selected a whippy branch, stripped it, and followed the herd.

"I'm gettin' some tired of eatin' dust," Arm said early that afternoon.

"Me, too," I said, "but I figured we'd make our move on the bay tomorrow."

"Why? It don' make no sense, Jake. They'll be fresh in the morning. Why not get a handle on that bay horse now an' tie him good for the night?"

I thought that over. Both Arm and I were fair-to-average ropers—we'd worked cattle when we couldn't find anything we could steal. Our plan was a simple one. We'd handle the horse the way a rank bull is handled. We'd each get ropes around his neck and allow him forty feet on either side. When he charged one of us—and he would charge—the other would haul him back. Like most plans it sounded a whole lot easier than it turned out to be.

We made our move, each of us riding up one side of the group of mares, loops ready. The bay stopped to face us, ears laid back tight to his skull, his lips curled back over his teeth.

The toughest part would be gettin' our ropes on him. Until we had him between he was free to tear us and our horses into pieces. I was on the right side of the herd and the stallion, Arm on the left. We both began drifting toward the bay. He was sharp enough to see what was coming and decided to fight right there rather than to attempt to run. He reared, front hooves flailing, snorting angrily.

I caught Arm's eye and nodded. We both headed for our quarry at a gallop, swinging wide loops.

The stallion didn't seem to know which of us to fight. After a moment he made his decision and charged me, running toward my galloping horse. I swung in a skidding turn and made my throw when the bay was ten feet or so from me. My roped bounced off his side and dropped to the ground. Armando did better. He dropped a loop over the stud's head and cranked his horse back the way he'd come to break the stallion's charge. He was a little late. My horse lost a good patch of coat and flesh from his hindquarter.

The stud hit the end of Arm's rope and was flipped onto his back and side, but was on his feet in the smallest part of a second. I'd been scrambling to hold my horse steady and get my rope back. I came up from behind the bay, who was concentrating on Armando, and made my second throw. This time I snared him and cut sharply back, dragging him out of his charge at Arm.

Both Arm and I hustled to the ends of our

ropes. It may have been a mistake but we'd both tied down what's called "hard an' fast"—meaning we'd secured the ends of our ropes to our saddle horns. In ranch work a cowhand'll take a couple of wraps around his saddle horn, but wants the rope to be free in case of some major blowup.

The stud was confused and madder than a rogue bull being threatened. We'd put a choking cloud of dust and grit in the air during our battle and my eyes were watering and at times I could barely see to the end of my rope.

We wanted to avoid the stud going down. If he did he could roll against the ropes and tangle up a leg or two, ending up with at least one broken leg. We fought back and forth for what seemed like forever but was actually maybe an hour or so. All three horses were dripping sweat, and so were Arm and I. All of us were coughing from the cloud we'd raised.

When I was dragging the stud my way, Arm got a loop around his rear feet and pulled back against me and my horse, leaving us with a crazed stallion stretched out between a pair of fatigued men and horses. It was a real good throw by Arm. He'd been a heeler on a couple of ranches and always carried two ropes. A heeler is the guy who gets a loop on the back legs of a calf in conjunction with a header, who ropes the front end, so that the calf can be branded right where he's stretched between the two ropers.

Trussing that bay horse up so he couldn't go anywhere was a job and a half. Our horses stood, holding the ropes tight, but that stud's head was mostly free and he snapped at us so violently that when his teeth crashed together, they sounding like a sprung bear trap. Arm got a short length of rope over the animal's snout and took a few wraps before tying it, eliminating the biting problem. Nevertheless the horse used his head and muzzle as a battering ram. A direct hit would break bones and shatter ribs.

I got rope around his front legs, secured it, and tied it off against the rope holding his rear legs together. We checked all the knots and ropes carefully—we didn't want to have to battle this ol' boy again. When we were positive he could barely move, we went to our horses and freed the ropes from the saddle horns.

The mares, who'd stood around in a cluster, wide-eyed, watching the battle, seemed to lose interest once their leader was down. They grazed on what little grass there was, shagging flies with their tails, just as they normally would. The youngsters continued their games as if nothing out of the ordinary had transpired. Every so often the stallion would let go a loud and angry whinny and the heads of the others would turn to him. When nothing else happened, they turned away once again.

Arm and I rode back to the water hole we'd crossed earlier and let our horses drink. Neither of us had used the branches we cut, which we'd tucked into our rifle scabbards along with our 30.30s. We threw the branches away, drank, picked up some dry limbs, refilled our canteens, and rode back to the herd. We set up a quick camp and started a fire. The mares wouldn't like the smoke, but they wouldn't go anywhere without their leader. Me an' Arm said we'd be damned if we would go without coffee after a day like we'd had. I emptied what was left in my flask into our cups. There wasn't much, but it was better than nothing. We ate jerky, which was also better than nothing, but not by much.

"We gonna have to wrestle with that sumbitch all over again *mañana*," Arm said. "He's a tough boy, okay. Couple times I was worried he would pull my horse off his feet."

"We don't have real far to take him," I said. "An' I suspect that he's smart enough to settle down when he sees he can't win this round. Workin' him in the corral ain't goin' to be a Sunday school picnic, though."

"Ees a good thing we planted the snubbing pole damn near to hell."

"Yep. He might bust me up, but he's not about to move that pole. An' all I gotta do is get to where I can handle and lead him—it's not like I'm breaking a saddle horse. I wouldn't ride him even if I could—not with that foot of his. The weight of a rider would throw him off balance."

Armando's response was a long, wet snore.

We fought with that beast most of the next morning. The weather had cooled that night and there was a stiff and chilly breeze blowing, raising yet more of a cloud of soil and sand around us as we tried to move the stud forward.

About midafternoon, the bay discovered that if he took steps in the direction we wanted him to go, the tension of the ropes around his neck would be lessened. He was still shaking his head, snorting, and slamming those teeth together—

but he was walking between our two horses. The mares, somewhat confused, followed us, I guess because most of them had followed the bay all their lives and he was moving now, so it was natural for them to plod along after him.

There were a few mares that didn't look bad, but there didn't seem to be a good chest or straight leg and sloped pastern among them. Many had scars from fights and more than a few were missing ears. The scars stood out against their coats like thick red worms, mostly near their withers and neck. I looked them over for a good long time before I shouted over to Arm, "I can't see feedin' this herd. There ain't anything here we'd breed to."

"Ees true," Arm yelled back to me, "but if we try to run them off now the stud, he go crazy—an' the mares, too."

"We can break them up and run them after we get the bay in the corral."

"Might be a couple worth keepin'."

"I guess we'll see."

We covered ground in spite of the slow pace. We picked up our packer and I tied him off on my saddle horn. He'd apparently enjoyed his vacation—all the grass was eaten right down to the dirt and he looked good—might even have put on a few pounds, given the fact that he had no work to do.

Every now an' again, the stallion would try to make a break, but Arm and I had gotten awful handy at hauling him in between us. For fifteen minutes after he'd attempted escape, the bay would whinny and rear and strike, even do some bucking, much like a kid having a tantrum.

There was a full moon that night, and the stars seemed close enough to the ground to be lanterns.

"Arm," I called, "what say we keep on rollin'? We'll make the ranch by midmorning tomorrow."

"*Bueno.* You see, each step brings me closer to the tequila in the cabinet."

I laughed. "I could use a snort or two my own-self."

My estimate of midmorning was overly optimistic, but we pulled in to our ranch well before dark.

We'd built the corral we were going to use to get a handle on stallions extra stout, and five feet taller than the other corrals. There was a wide, nicely reinforced gate we'd latched wide-open, which was a good move on our part. It could have been real tough getting close enough to unlatch the gate with the stud acting up.

Armando banged his heels against his horse's sides and the black leaped forward, putting lots of pressure on the bay. I dropped my rope, jumped down from my saddle, and ran to the gate. I swung it closed just as Arm galloped out. The stallion stood in the corral near the snubbing post with a pair of forty-foot ropes still around his neck. He looked more confused than anything else. I'd expected a blowup when he figured out that he was boxed in by fences too high to jump, and would start raising general hell, trying to kick his way out of the enclosure. Instead, he merely stood there, looking around. I suppose he was as tired as we and our horses were.

The mares, too, were confused. They whinnied

out to the bay, and when he responded they approached the corral. There were as skittish as deer and didn't dare come too close, but hearing their boss seemed to comfort them some. They ran out in a group about a hundred yards into a pasture and began to graze.

We took our horses into the barn and spent some time rubbing them down, checking and cleaning their hooves, and putting a ration of molasses-rich crimped oats in front of them in their stalls, along with buckets of fresh water. They'd done fine work for us and they deserved a little extra time. Anyway, it's a code in the West that a man takes care of his critters before he takes care of himself.

There was a large meat pie on our little kitchen table, covered with a couple of layers of cheesecloth to keep the flies away.

"Them women—I love them," Armando said, tossing the cheesecloth aside, and picking up one of the big wooden spoons placed next to the pie. I did the same. We ate the entire thing in a matter of minutes.

"How about we hire those two to cook and kinda clean up around here? Neither one of us are much good at that stuff."

"*Bueno*. We pay them well, no?"

"Absolutely."

Armando pushed his chair back and headed for the tequila cabinet. He took out a quart, yanked the cork with his teeth, and said, "Les' go out an' see what the bay horse is doing." He took a monumental swig of the booze, belched, and handed the bottle to me.

"We need some glasses. We're like a pair of stumblebums sucking whiskey out of bottles," I said, after taking a long hit.

"Blanca y Teresa will get some, we ask them to. Me—I don' need no glass."

"I'll set up an account at the mercantile an' they can get whatever they want," I said. "Come to think of it, we don't have any plates or such—spoons and knives an' forks."

"If you gettin' glasses, you might as well get the whole wagonload a that horseshit, no?"

Armando wasn't big on the social niceties. His sheath knife was two utensils rolled into one piece—knife and fork. He didn't need a spoon—soup or stew he simply drank from the bowl.

We stopped at the barn and picked up a flake of hay. When we got to the corral I tossed the hay over the top and then Arm and I climbed to the top rail. The stallion was lathered and sweat dripped from his chest and sides. He'd obviously been running—and running hard. He ignored the hay. I noticed he'd drunk about half of the water in the trough at one corner of the corral. He stood and glared at us, and it seemed that his glare could melt steel.

The mares had moved a bit farther away but we could still see them dotting the pasture. When the bay whinnied they no longer answered.

The bay lurched into a run again, moving as fast as his tanglefoot allowed him to, following the fence line around and around again. The two ropes flailed behind him, like snakes chasing him in his headlong dash. When he came by us we could hear the deep bellows-like sound of a horse that's been run too long.

He made another half circuit of the corral, stopped, and then ran directly at us. "I hope the fence is as stout as we think," Arm said, " 'cause he ain't gonna stop."

We pulled our legs to the outside. The horse bashed into the fence with his chest, his head turned aside, teeth clattering together. He was squealing madly, crazily, forelegs now attacking the air next to him. He'd lost control of his urine in his wrath and a heavy, pungent reek of ammonia rose up around him. The fence held. I reached out and got my hand under one of the loops around his neck and when he backed off, I brought the rope in.

"Maybe we'd best let him be for a couple of days," I said, "until he settles a little."

He rushed us again, flailing hell out of the fence just below us with his front hooves, doing his best to get his teeth into us.

"*Sí*. He will tire of this running an' biting shit before long."

We each took another swig of tequila.

"You notice how the horse, he tracks? Back hoof striking where front one was?"

"Yeah, I did notice. An' did you see how he carried his head at the gallop? He's one proud sumbitch."

"*Sí*. Is true. But, my pardner . . ." Arm stopped midthought and lifted the bottle to his mouth.

"What? What's the problem?"

Arm thought for a long moment. "Look," he

said, and his words were quick and tumbled over one another. "Theese goddamn horse, he weel kill you, Jake. You think you can ride or break any animal an' you're way wrong."

"Horseshit. I know when to let go, Arm. Like that hellfire bitch I rode down in—where? Yuma? She wanted to kill me an' I rode her 'til she couldn't stand."

"I made money on that ride, Jake."

"For or against?"

"For."

"You took a chance, Armando."

"Ever'thing we do is a chance, no? Hell, tha's the way we live. But it don' mean you gotta get killed by a crazy horse."

"I'll take it slow an' easy," I said. "You worry too much."

"Boolshit." We each had a taste of the tequila. "What say we ride into town, see Tiny, hire on Teresa an' Blanca?"

"An' a cold beer?"

"You bet."

I coiled the rope and we walked to the barn to saddle our horses. I hung the rope from a hook near the big front doors. A man can't tell when he's going to need a throwing rope in a big hurry—particularly cattlemen, but the same thing applies to horse traders and breeders.

We took it easy on the way to Hulberton. The temperature was more fall-like than we'd been experiencing, and it felt good—the air was cool and fresh.

We heard the ringing of Tiny's hammer against

his anvil from way far out. It sounded a bit like a bell.

"That sound," Arm said, "mus' carry on forever, no? To the moon an' past it."

"Maybe so. You know how a gunshot sounds a little fuzzy from far off? An anvil doesn't do that—the sound stays clear."

"Es verdad."

Tiny was just finishing shoeing a nice-looking carriage mare. He nodded but didn't speak because he had a half dozen horseshoe nails in his mouth, head pointing out. The horse stood well as Tiny tapped the nails home. The six points protruded a half inch above the top of the hoof and Tiny snipped those off with a sharpened plier-like tool. His final step was to flatten the metal studs left behind on the hoof surface to snug the shoe. He eased the mare's foot to the floor and straightened.

"I hear-tell you boys got yourself a stud horse," Tiny said.

"How the hell did you know that? We haven't told . . ."

"Ain't no secrets 'round here, boys. Fella by the name of Les Auborn—a patent medicine drummer—seen you with the horse between you on ropes. Les, he said the horse was a good looker."

"He's that, okay," I said. "What else he is we don't know yet."

"A man might get thirsty shoein' a horse, no?" Arm said.

Tiny took off his muleskin apron and set it

aside. He led the mare to a stall and closed her in. He rubbed her snout before walking to us. "What's keepin' us?" he said, grinning.

On the way to the saloon I explained our plan to hire Teresa and Blanca.

"You want them to live in or come back an' forth each day?"

"I never thought about it. We've got enough bedrooms, so they might just as well live at the ranch, if they want to do that. We'll pay 'em good, an' the work ain't half bad—cleanin', cooking, an' such like."

"They live above the dry goods store," Tiny said. "You more'n likely can catch them there now."

"I'll go," Arm said. "I have Spanish. You boys go ahead, but make sure you save some beer for me." He turned to me. "What will we pay?"

I looked at Tiny. "Twenty a week, each?"

"Damn," he said, "that's more than a good cowhand draws. Them ladies'll jump on it."

We separated, Arm walking toward the dry goods store and Tiny and I to the saloon. There were a bunch of horses tied outside, and lots of noise from inside, considering it was barely noon.

"The KG boys just dropped a thousand head at the railroad yards," Tiny said. "They've got money in their pockets an' they're thirsty an' horny."

As we approached the bat wings a lanky fellow with a nose gushing blood came out as if he were flying—a good couple of feet above the ground. He hit about eight feet out, moaned, turned over, and went to sleep.

As we walked in, a 'hand drew his Colt and

put a couple of slugs into the ceiling. That kind of gave his pals an idea and within seconds the place sounded like a shooting gallery at a county fair. There were thirty or so men crowding the bar. Some showed signs of a very recent bath, a haircut and new clothes; the rest looked about like you'd expect a man to look after over a month on the range, driving a thousand head of beef.

There were three bartenders and all of them were running their asses off, trying to keep up with shouted orders from the cowboys. They were also pocketing money the cowhands didn't owe—snagging a five-dollar note for a single beer, clearing off the change in front of other men who were too drunk to see what was happening.

Tiny and I stood just inside the bat wings. My hand dropped to the grips of my Colt on its own—I didn't tell it to do so.

Tiny leaned in close to me and shouted into my ear, "They're harmless, Jake. Drunk an' stupid, but they wouldn't draw on a man. Shit, if I followed cows' asses for a month or better, I'd be raisin' hell, too."

We shoved our way to the bar. One tender recognized Tiny and came right over.

"Six beers," Tiny shouted. "We got a friend coming."

"Lookit, Tiny," the bartender said, "the owner has jacked the prices of beer an' booze and . . ."

I placed a twenty-dollar gold piece on the bar. "Keep 'em coming," I said.

The whores were doing lots of business; no sooner would a soiled dove come down the stairs than she'd be escorted back up by another cowboy. A couple of minor fistfights broke out about who was next, but nothing serious.

The beer tasted real good.

Armando came in, a big smile on his face, and pushed his way to me an' Tiny.

"The ladies, they'll be out tomorrow," he said. "They'll be ready to move in—a friend will bring them and their things on a farm wagon."

I shouted into Arm's ear, "There's no supplies for them—nothing for them to cook. How can . . ."

"I give them one hundred dollar, *mi hermano*. They'll buy what they want at the mercantile. That's why they needed the wagon—to haul all that stuff to the ranch."

"I hope you told them to stock up on beef-steaks," I said.

"For sure, no? I tol' them we like to eat steak for every meal, an' we like them rare an'—"

"Now, lookit this," a cowboy yelled. "We're drinkin' with a goddamn beaner."

"Ahh, shit," Tiny said.

Armando wasn't a man to do much talking before a fight. He buried his fist in the cowhand's gut, and caught the guy's face with his knee as he crumpled forward. Those who were standing close enough heard the snap of cartilage. Of course, a dozen 'hands moved in to get their hands on Arm. Tiny stepped forward and so did I. Tiny grabbed the cowboy closest to him, slammed the man's face into the bar, lifted him and threw him back into the crowd.

Two cowboys came after me. I kicked one in the balls and got a good haymaker into the second fellow's jaw, and he went down.

Tiny was throwing cowhands around and enjoying every second of it. Someone would take a swing at him and his grin would broaden and he'd pick up his opponent by the neck and belt and hurl him back into the crowd.

Arm was doing a hell of a job, too. His face was cut up a bit and his nose was bleeding, but he was taking on all comers and dropping them like stones down a well.

When the first shot was fired, the fistfighting stopped. Men with fists drawn back and ready to deliver halted in midmotion. The crowd spread out, leaving an open tunnel between Armando and the boy who fancied himself a gunfighter.

"You don' need to do this," Arm said in the eerie silence that had come about.

"I don'," the kid mocked. "Maybe I want to. See, I don't like you goddamn beaners."

Arm let his hand drop to his side, inches from his holster.

I tried to step between them, trying to reason with the kid, but Tiny pulled me back. "Ain't no stoppin' it now," he said. "Is Arm handy with his Colt?"

"He'll do," I said.

The kid may have been twenty years old—or maybe not. He'd been on the drive, but he didn't seem to be drunk. He wore his holster at his waist, like a farmer or a cowhand, and he was facing Armando full-on. He was no gunfighter—he was a kid, is all.

Arm turned to his side and crouched down a bit.

"You goddamn beaners are scum," the kid said, "and so are your whore mothers."

"Ahhh, shit," Tiny said again.

"Theese is wrong," Arm said. "You can no talk about my mother. It is not allowed. You see?"

"Theese? Can no?"

"You mus' not do this. You'll die, boy. I know how to fight with guns—an' you don't. Turn away, kid. Please."

The kid stood stock-still for a long moment and then his right hand reached down and grabbed the grips of his pistol. He drew and had his weapon out and was raising it toward Arm.

My partner drew and fired twice, one shot hitting the kid in the throat, the second next to his nose. He went down immediately and he was no doubt dead before he hit the floor.

Arm stood there with his pistol hanging at his side. He was pale and I saw the hand holding his Colt was trembling a bit.

"I din' want to keel him," he said quietly, maybe so quietly that only Tiny and I could hear.

I took his gun from his hand and dropped it into his holster.

"Come on, Arm, we gotta go back to the ranch."

"I tried to let him stop the fight," Arm said. "I tried, you know?"

"Yeah. I know. Come on, pardner."

We picked up our horses at Tiny's place and rode home. Neither of us spoke. There was really nothing to say.

Chapter Four

As we were unsaddling in the barn, Armando turned to me. "Ees the same thing," he said, as if he were continuing a conversation.

"What's the same thing?"

"That kid you killed an' this boy I killed today. They poosh an' poosh an' end up dead. We are not big guns, *mi hermano*. Why come we to these gunfight?"

"I suppose anybody who can draw and not shoot themselves in the foot is a big gun in Hulberton, Arm. But today—that was a thing about your race, your family. And you're right—the kid pushed and pushed. You did nothing wrong."

"Doesn't make the boy less dead."

"No, it don't. But I've been thinkin' on something. Maybe when we get the Busted Thumb up an' running, we can put our guns away for good."

Arm thought for a long time before turning away from me. "It won' ever happen," he said quietly. "We will live an' die with our guns on."

Tiny showed up the next day driving a farm wagon loaded with Teresa and Blanca and their belongings and things for the home. It looked like they'd spent the whole hundred Arm gave them. There were fifty-pound sacks of coffee, salt, sugar, flour, a couple of canned hams, lots of canned peaches and pears, as well as some restaurant-type dishes and knives, forks, and spoons. Other boxes and bags held stuff we didn't bother to look into. The women scurried about, from the wagon up the stairs to their room and then from the wagon to the big walk-in pantry in the kitchen.

Tiny, Arm, and I sat on the porch and rolled smokes. When all our cigarettes were lit and drawing nicely, Tiny said, "You boys are gonna need grain. I got a pal at the mill who can get what you want within a few days."

"Might just as well stock up with winter comin'," I said. "How about a thousand pounds of crimped oats with a molasses cut, a thousand of corn, and a thousand of crimped oats without the molasses. The days we gotta keep them in, they'll go nuts not bein' able to run off the energy that molasses generates." I handed four twenties to Tiny.

"You ain't sayin' much, Arm," Tiny said.

"No. I ain't."

"He's still chewin' on that kid he dropped yesterday," I said.

"Well, hell," Tiny said. "He didn't have no choice. The kid was bound an' determined to shoot himself a Mex—don' matter if it was Armando or Santana. An' that stuff about Arm's people—I woulda did the same thing. Somebody woulda put a few rounds into the little bastard sooner or later."

Armando nodded but didn't speak.

An uncomfortable silence followed. Then Tiny said, "I got a fella bringin' in a half dozen mares in the next couple of days. I ain't sure what they are, but this fella, he's never done me wrong. It'd be worth a ride for you boys to town to check them out. Like I said, I don't know what they are, but my pal don't try to unload coyote feed on me."

"We'll do that, Tiny."

"When you gonna start workin' that stud horse?"

"I kinda thought I'd play a bit with him today, get his rope around the snubbin' post, see if I can't handle him a little bit."

Before long, Tiny went on his way and the women banged and clattered about in the house. I went in for some coffee and saw they had a metal bathing tub—it looked like a stock trough, only smaller. There was a cauldron of water boiling on the stove and a long-handled brush and a lump of soap on the floor next to the tub.

"What's . . ." I began.

"You an' Armando, you steenk," Blanca said, using more English than I thought she had. I guess lots of Mexicans ran that ploy to avoid arguments or controversy with Anglos. "You will have bath."

"The hell I will," I said. "I been rained on plenty in the last few weeks. An' this bath stuff is unhealthy—it makes a man's skin soft and sets him up for cholera."

"You first," Blanca said, "then Armando."

Teresa poured the last cauldron of water into the already half-filled tub while Blanca fetched a coarse towel for me.

"I ain't . . ."

"You don't take no bath, you don' eat," Blanca said, stone-faced. The two women left the room. "Shit," I said. Then I shucked down. Actually, the hot water felt pretty good, and the grayish brown soil and dried sweat that rose from my body indicated that perhaps the ladies were right. I set to with that brush an' soap until my skin tingled, an' I washed an' rinsed my hair, too. The damned towel felt like a feed sack, but at least it dried me off. I dressed an' called the women. "All done."

They came into the kitchen, looked me over, an' nodded. *"Es bueno,"* Teresa said. "We will buy new clothes next time in town. Yours are but rags."

I couldn't argue with her on that point.

"You send Armando in now," Blanca instructed. "He, too, is a peeg."

I went out to the barn to pick up my throwing rope. Arm was rubbing saddle soap into the fenders of his saddle.

"The women need you inside right now," I said.

"For what?"

"Ask them. I got a horse to play with."

"I'll see what it is they want an' then come to the corral to watch, maybe help, no?"

"Fine with me."

I put my arm through my coiled rope and rather than using the gate, climbed over the fence into the corral. The bay stud was chewing away at a flake of hay I'd tossed over to him early that morning. His head snapped up and he glared at me, huffing through his nose—challenging me. He'd worked off the rope that'd been around his neck, which I hadn't expected. He must have rubbed his head an' neck against the side of his water trough or somehow hung up the rope on a rough board of the fence. I let my rope slide down into my hands, coils in the left, loop in the right.

The horse watched my every move, his eyes embers, his muscles tight, ready to fight. Rather than approach him, I walked the circuit of the corral—slowly, taking short steps and making no fast motions. His hay and where he stood was maybe fifteen feet from the fence. He moved his body to watch me walking, but didn't offer to charge me, although I could tell he was considering doing so. I knew he'd do it eventually. There was no doubt about that.

I kept on walking 'round and 'round that corral for a good long time at the same slow pace. The bay's eyes and mine remained locked, even as he lowered his head to grab hay. He seemed to quiet a bit—his muscles didn't seem quite as rigid, but he never stopped looking at me.

I'd been very slowly—a quarter inch at a time— letting my loop grow until I had it about as wide around as a half keg, which should be all I needed if I made a good throw.

The stallion's eyes flicked to Arm as he climbed up an' sat on the top rail, watching. Obviously, he knew enough not to say anything or make any quick moves—he was damned near as good a horseman as I was.

I stepped out a yard or so from the fence and kept walking at the same pace. The bay's ears lay back immediately. He'd noticed the change.

When I saw his chest swell, I braced myself and lifted my loop. The stallion charged, nostrils flared, teeth bared, a long string of saliva hanging from his mouth. I raised my loop and whirled it once—but the horse didn't give me a chance to use it. He veered very sharply to his right and hit the fence where Arm's legs had been, bashing the boards the way a runaway locomotive would hit a solid wall. I heard Arm from the other side grumble, "Crazy goddamn horse."

I scrambled for the fence and was up and over it before I looked back. The stallion was staring hotly, piercingly, at the spot where Arm had been. If I hadn't run, I could have put a rope on him and snugged it to the post right then. *Shit!*

Armando's hair was still wet from his bath, I noticed, and I grinned. "I wasn't sure I recognized you with all the dirt gone," I said.

"Me? You look like a banker, Jake."

We walked to the barn. "He's one sneaky sumbitch," Arm said. "His eyes were on you 'til the very last second."

"I coulda gotten a rope on him if I hadn't skedaddled."

"*Sí.* An' the *perro*—the dog—he woulda caught the rabbit if he no stop to take a sheet, no?"

I laughed. "I guess. But I'll get him to the post. I'm goin' to go out an' just walk again later, carryin' my rope."

"You sure this boy is the stud we're after?" Arm asked.

"Well, name a confirmation fault other than that twisted-up foot."

There was a long silence. "Ain't none."

"There ya go, Arm."

Arm changed the subject. "You was lookin' him straight in the eye, no? You know this is the challenge, 'specially to the wild one—an' this mustang, he's as wild as a box of rattlesnakes."

"I wanted to challenge him. I need his respect. I'm never going to break him to saddle, so I gotta get him to respect me."

Later that afternoon I climbed the fence, my rope in my right hand, coiled without a loop, and a thick flake of hay under my arm. I tossed the hay so that it landed about ten feet from the snubbing post. I knew the horse was hungry; there wasn't a scrap of his morning hay left. I began my walking. The bay alternately eyed me and eyed the hay. At that point, my right hand gripping my rope was sweating—I didn't know if he was going to eat or attack. The only weapon I had was my rope, but a well-placed blow with a coiled rope on a horse's muzzle could change his mind in a hurry about what he wanted to do.

After what seemed like a century, he walked, stiff-legged, ears back, to the hay. I made three more circuits of the corral and then climbed up on the fence to sit next to Arm and watched the bay go after the fresh hay.

It was then we saw the two riders heading our way. Arm and I jumped down. These two fellows were scruffy and dirty—they looked like saddle tramps. They were both lean, with many days of unshaved beard. They drew rein in front of us but didn't dismount.

"Quite a 'stang you got there," one said to me. "We seen him real good from up on the hill beyond the corral. He's pretty 'nough for a dozen mustangs, 'cept for that tanglefoot."

"Something we can do for you boys?" I said.

"Well, truth is, we're lookin' for some ranch work. We can do most anything. We been workin' cattle an' horses lately."

I looked more closely at them. Their horses were ribby and showed spur marks. "Horses an' cattle, huh? Seems strange neither one of you has a rope on your saddle."

The talker forced a laugh. "Damndest thing," he said, "we tied up at a gin mill in the last town we passed an' some fool stole our ropes."

"But lef' your rifles and bedrolls, eh?" Arm said, derision dripping from his voice.

"You listen here, Pancho—we . . ."

"Get off our property or we'll blow holes in you," I said. "We don't need scum like you around."

They looked at each other for a moment. Arm was off to my left. I'd dropped my rope at my feet when the two men rode up, leaving my right hand free. I didn't need to look at my partner to know he was ready for whatever happened.

"Well, shit," the talker said, turning his horse, "you sure ain't civil here. Didn't even offer a cup of coffee. I think what we'll do is ride on."

"That's a fine idea," I said.

"One can tell the quality of a man by the way he treats his horse," Arm said, probably loud enough for the men to hear. Neither responded.

Later on that afternoon I half filled a bucket with crimped oats and humped over the fence to walk my circuit. The bay hustled to the far side of the fence, leaving his hay. I set the bucket down about five feet from the post and then walked around the periphery of the corral again. This time the stud was much faster in getting over to see what had been left for him. His ears were still back, but he didn't offer to charge me again. I climbed over the fence, sat for a bit, watching him bury his muzzle in the bucket. If there's one thing all horses love, it's oats—particularly when the shell is broken—crimped—for them.

Armando was sitting at the kitchen table with two glasses and a bottle of tequila. I sat across from him and he poured two hefty shots into each glass. "He like the oats, no?" Arm said.

"Sure. An' he didn't pay as much attention to me when I was walkin' around the corral."

"Ees good."

"Damn right it is. Tomorrow morning I'm going to rope him, snub him down, leave him maybe eight, ten feet, an' get the hell outta there. Then I'll continue feeding him for a few days."

"He ain' stupid," Arm said. "He'll soon learn who brings the groceries."

"That's what I'm countin' on," I said.

The sky was gray the next morning and there was the smell of snow in the air. From atop the fence I could see a farm wagon loaded with sacks of grain headed toward us, the two draft horses pulling it sweating into their harnesses because of the weight. I waved to the driver and he waved back. I formed a loop, made sure I had a good hold on the bucket of grain I carried, and jumped down to the inside of the corral. The bay was standing out from the far fence a few yards, which I thought was a good sign.

I set the bucket down maybe five feet from the snubbin' post. I noticed the bucket from the day before had been kicked across the corral to where it lay, one side caved in. I began my walk. The horse watched me for a bit but was more interested in looking at the bucket. I glanced up. Arm sat on the top rail, a rope in hand.

After I'd made a couple of circuits the horse eased on over to the new bucket. I was maybe twenty feet away from him, on his left. I knew he was watching me—and I knew he wanted those oats.

Well, hell, I'm probably not going to get a better shot than this. 'Course if I miss, it's a long haul to the fence, an' then I gotta climb the sumbitch. But I'm not goin' to miss.

I didn't need to shake out my loop; it was already formed and ready. I faced the bay and took my throw. It was a perfect toss, I don't mind sayin'. It slapped against his head and settled around his neck. I started haulin' ass as soon as the loop left my hand, what was left of the coil in my hand. The horse stood there as if in shock for a moment—which gave me time to wind a half dozen turns of rope around the snubbing post. He backed up quickly, was stopped by the rope, and lit out toward me, ready to chew and stomp me into paste.

I'm not much at running and Western boots with high riding heels, didn't add to my speed. But, I'll tell you what. I burned up the dirt getting to the fence, grabbed hold, flung myself up, and sat on the rail to see what would happen.

The bay hit the end of the rope when I was

about halfway to the fence—and the momentum—the force behind his charge—flipped him up into the air, all four feet going out from under him. He slammed to the ground on his back and was up immediately, rearing, squealing, bucking, carrying on as if ol' Satan was nibbling on his ass. He tried a run in a different direction and it ended, 'course, in the same way the first had. He was already sweating and trembling with anger. He tried bucking and lunging again but the rope stopped him each time. He battled that rope for a good half hour until sweat dripped from his flanks, belly, and chest and he stood blowing, sucking air. I stayed where I was on the fence and rolled a smoke. Maybe forty-five minutes later, the stallion walked to the bucket and dropped his nose into it. I jumped down on the outside of the fence as did Arm. We grinned at each other.

"Step one," I said.

For the next few days I did nothing with him except carry out a flake of hay, retrieve the empty bucket, replace it with a new one—crimped oats and molasses, thanks to our delivery from town—and walk back to the fence. He'd stopped booting the buckets after the first one for whatever reasons he had. That kinda surprised me.

I talked all the while I did my chores with him. Arm's and mine were probably the first human voices the bay horse had ever heard, and I wanted him to get used to the sounds men make. Sometimes I sang: *Buffalo Gals*, *When Johnny Comes Marchin' Home*, *Oh, Susanna*, and such like. Mostly, though, I talked. Arm spent some time in nonsense talk with our horse in both Spanish and English.

Every so often the stud would try the rope, but without the frenzied attack he'd shown the first time. I guess he grew weary of being jacked off his feet and bashed down to the ground.

Meanwhile, we had to find some mares good enough to match our stallion. We went into town to see if Tiny had heard anything and we put up some posters seeking good, solid, young but broke-to-handling mares. We had time and a bundle of money. We weren't worrying about it.

Teresa and Blanca were working out beautifully. Breakfast, for instance consisted of a dozen or so eggs for us to split up, a pile of fried potatoes, and slabs of hog side meat. Lunch was just as good, but wider in scope. We even had soup one day. Supper they went all out for: steaks as big as saddle blankets, fluffy mashed spuds, fresh baked bread, and all the coffee we could drink. At supper they always put our bottle of tequila on the table, too. They kept the place spotless. The house always had that clean, fresh aroma of wood polish floating through it. Blanca drifted through the kitchen one morning to ask when we were next going to town.

"We were thinking 'bout goin' in today," I said. "Why?"

"There are tings we need. I make a leest, okay?"

"Sure—that'll be fine."

Teresa looked around the corner. "You take the peckhorse, too, no?"

Arm sighed. "How much things do you need?"

he asked. "We both have saddlebags that'll carry plenty."

"Too small," Blanca said.

"You need peckhorse," Teresa added.

We saddled up and then put the rig on the packhorse. He was frisky and getting fat—he hadn't been used for a while. He got a little too cute with Arm's black and lost a mouthful of hair and hide. That calmed him down.

There was a wind that had a bite to it, and the temperature was low and dropping.

"Ain't summer no more," Arm said. He had the collar up on his heavy jacket, as did I.

We let our horses run a bit, holding them in so the pack animal could keep up. When we reined in after a mile or so, Arm said, "The stallion, he is coming good."

"Yeah. He is. He's still as wild as a hawk, but I can get next to him without him charging me or even laying his ears back."

"Would you breed him now?"

"Might be a little dicey, but yeah, I would—if it's the right mare an' she's in season. I'm sure our ol' boy would climb right on, but whether or not he'd do any biting that'd hurt the mare, I dunno."

"What means 'in season'?"

"Same thing as 'horsing'—or 'horny' for that matter. All ready for a stud."

"I know 'horny.' This 'season' thing is silly." He paused for a moment. "Maybe we need to tease him with a mare, see how he takes the scent, no?"

"Good idea." I didn't bother to tell my partner that was precisely what I intended to do.

We dropped off our packhorse at the mercantile, along with the list the ladies had prepared. I hadn't bothered to look at it—what they needed was what they need. I asked the clerk to wrap four quarts of good whiskey real careful-like and include those with the supplies, too. As I was leaving, I stopped at the door. "Put one of those quarts at the top of a load," I said. "We might give it a trial on the way home."

The wind was whipping bits of ice that stung our faces like bees as we rode down to Tiny's shop. He was hammering a fracture in a steel wheel rim as we tied our horses. His sale corral was full—he'd obviously made a sizable purchase lately. Arm and I stood at the fence, looking over the stock. Our eyes came to rest on the same horse: a buckskin mare that was the prettiest damned thing a man could ever see. Buckskins are eye-catchers anyway, but this gal was perfect. She stood square, looking about—curious, not frightened. Her coat was the color of homemade taffy and the dorsal line of black down her spine was straight and true. She had a good chest for a mare and her black mane and tail were long, without tangles. Her withers were prominent but not overly so, and her legs were picture-perfect, with gently sloping pasterns.

"Madre de Dios," Arm said.

"Yeah—she's somethin'."

Tiny set aside his wheel rim and greeted us. "You saw the buckskin, I see. I was gonna send a kid out to fetch you to eyeball that pretty li'l girl."

"Is she as good as she looks?" I asked.

"Better. Got the temperament of a new bride, reins great, backs away from fighting with the other mares. She's a good 'un, boys."

A one-horse carriage pulled up at the hitching rail. The driver—dressed like a banker or an undertaker—jumped down. He smacked Armando's horse on the ass to make room for his horse and rig. Arm started forward, but I held him back. "Let it go," I said. "The guy's a dude. Lookit the shine on them boots. He's never stepped in horseshit in his life."

The man approached us. "You are the owner of the horses out there?" he asked Tiny.

"Yeah. I am. Folks call me Tiny." The gent didn't offer his hand, nor did Tiny. "These two boys are Jake . . ."

The dude waved away that introduction with a choppy hand motion. "I've come to talk to you, not your stablehands. I'm interested in that buckskin. I saw her when you brought her in last night—and I saw one of your boys run her down the street this morning. She covers ground."

"You got a name?" Tiny asked.

"I'm Morgan Dansworth," he said. "You've no doubt heard of me. I have the biggest cattle and running horse operation in West Texas. That mare would make a good addition. If she's as fast as she looks, I'll race her. If not, she looks like a real good brood mare."

"I ain't heard of you," Tiny said.

"Me neither," Arm said.

"Nor me," I said.

Dansworth flushed slightly and his eyes squinted a bit. Like I said, he was dressed like a banker—fine suit, polished boots, fawn-colored gloves, a fur hat.

He cleared his throat, needlessly, I thought. "Be that as it may, I'll purchase that mare."

Tiny looked at Armando and me. I shook my head. "She ain't for sale," he said. "You're a little too late."

"The horse hasn't been here a full day yet! Who bought . . ."

"These two stablehands," Tiny said.

Dansworth forced a smile at us. "What'd you pay for the animal? I'll double the amount—right now, in cash. Certainly there are other horses here that're good enough for your purposes—whatever they may be."

"Like Tiny said," I said, "she ain't for sale."

"What we pay for her is no your business," Arm added.

Dansworth's face grew more red, and it wasn't from the wind. "I'll have that horse," he said. "I'll pay you three times what you—"

"She isn't for sale," I said, louder than I usually talk.

" 'Less you got other business here, I'll ask you to be on your way," Tiny said.

"An' you hit my horse again, you be swallowing your teeth, *pendejo.*"

"Like I said, I'll have that horse—one way or another. I have better than a hundred men working for me. Many are very tough. Better you sell now and avoid trouble."

"Trouble? Sheeee—it! You bring it right on!" Arm said. "We own the Busted Thumb Horse Ranch—even a fancy prancer like you could find us."

Dansforth glared at Tiny for a long moment. "You'll regret this," he said.

"I don' think so."

The dude untied his horse, climbed onto his carriage, swung it around, and took off at a run. "You see the bit in that carriage horse's mouth? One of them spade Mex things—sorry, Arm— that'll rip hell outta a horse's mouth," Tiny said.

"Because I am Mexican does not mean I ruin animals," Arm said.

"I know that."

"*Bueno.*"

"What do you need for the mare?" I asked.

"Hundred and a half."

Arm whistled.

"Sold," I said. "Will you hold her for a day or so?" I dug into my pants and started counting out money. "I don't have but eighty with me," I said. "Arm, you got . . ."

"Cut the horseshit, boys. The mare is yours. Bring me the money in a day or so—I know you're good for it."

"*Sí,*" Arm said. "We are also good for some of them cold beers an' maybe a taste of whiskey to warm the blood, no?"

"Fine idea," Tiny said. "Let's do it."

We sat at a table in the saloon. Most of the cowhands had cleared out—either lost all their money to the professional gamblers, spent it on whores and booze, or simply moved on.

"I know Dansworth—or I know of him, any- way," Tiny said. "He's got some fine racehorses, I'll give him that. Not just hotbloods, either—all kinds." He paused. "I heard that fancy Colt he carries was made by a gunsmith in Chicago—starting from scratch. Then, Danworth spent a few months with a 'ol boy named Jackson—a gunfighter—an' learned to use the pistol. Word says he's fast an' deadly, dude or not."

The bartender was familiar with our needs. He brought over a tray with six schooners of beer and three double-shots of whiskey.

"What else do you know?" I asked.

Tiny downed his whiskey.

"Well, his papa built up a hell of a operation durin' the war, sellin' beef to both the Yanks an' the rebs. Made him real rich. He was a horseman—knew horses and always had prime stock around—and always lookin' for more to buy. He up an' croaked three, four years ago an' his kid took over. That cowflop we just saw was the kid. Thing is, he's got those hundred men an' more, an' he uses them like a army."

My whiskey was raw, but the warmth of it going down felt good. "You think we got anything to worry about from him?"

"We step on that *cucaracha*, no?"

"Sure. But he ain't the one you gotta worry about. It's his men. From what I heard, he's got a pack of deserters, crazies, an' gunslingers ridin' for him. He pays them good an' they ain't afraid to trade gunfire."

"Neither are we," I said.

"I know that. All I'm sayin' is to keep your eyes open an' watch that mare real close. By the way—how's the stud comin'?"

"He's doin good, considerin' he was as wild as

a damned mountain cat when we brought him in. I've got him snubbed an' I can touch his muzzle."

"I'd say don't push him, Jake. Take your time."

Arm laughed. "Jake, he's as patient as a kid at *Navidad*."

Tiny changed the subject. "How're Blanca an' Teresa doin'?"

"They're great. God, the way they feed us. I swear to you, Tiny, it won't be long before I'm as fat as Armando."

"Ees muscle, no fat."

We all hefted our beers, laughing. Arm held up his whiskey glass and the tender brought over another trio of doubles. After we'd all finished our drinks we went back to Tiny's shop. We stopped at the corral to gawk at the buckskin mare for a bit, and then Arm an' me rode over to the mercantile. Our packhorse was tied to the hitching rail in front. The poor critter was as loaded as he could be, but there didn't seem to be much weight to what he carried in his bags—just size and bulk. I went in to even up. The price was $47.34, which is a pretty stiff amount of money, but what the hell.

The stuff that'd been minute ice particles had turned to snow as we wet our whistles in the saloon. There was some wind behind the snow, but visibility wasn't too bad. We rode at a walk. At one point I reined in, swung down, and stepped over to the packhorse at the end of the rope wrapped around my saddle horn. The clerk had done what I asked; there was a bottle of whiskey carefully wrapped in a grain sack and brown paper.

"This will warm us up a bit," I said to Armando.

We got to the ranch just before dark and tied the packhorse to the rail in front of the porch. Then we saw to our own horses, rubbing them down, graining them, filling their buckets with fresh water. When we got back to the house, the packhorse had been unloaded and he stood there looking hungry. "You go on in," I said to Arm. "I'll look to this guy—give him a little treat."

Although he wasn't sweated at all, I rubbed him down and gave him a bucket of molasses grain and another of fresh water. Arm's and my horse picked up the scent of the molasses immediately and started nickering and carrying on for their share. "Hush, you silly bastards," I told them. "You didn't carry nothing but a couple of men. This fella carried everything the ladies wanted." I picked a nice leather halter an' brought it into the house with me.

It was warm in the kitchen and there was a good fire in the living room. Blanca and Teresa fed us our usual steaks, potatoes, and some cut carrots as a special treat. After we ate we moved out to the living room to watch the fire.

There's something hypnotic about watching a good fire burn. It takes a man away, deep into his thoughts—his good thoughts—and makes him feel at peace with the universe.

I found my eyes closed and my chin on my chest and decided to head up to bed.

"Put your clothes outside your door," Teresa said. "We take care of them."

I entered my room. On my bed were brand-new denim pants and a nice work shirt, along with socks and long johns. I moved that stuff to the floor, stripped, put my old clothes outside my door, and climbed into my bed. I heard Armando come up the stairs and then, a few minutes later, the soft steps of one of the women. After that I heard nothing.

The next morning I looked out my door, expecting to see my washed clothes. There was nothing there. The space in front of Arm's door was bare, too.

"Hey!" I called. "Where are our duds?"

Blanca came to the stairs and glared up at me. "Those was rags. They smelled like the peeg pen. Some we cut for washing cloths, the other we burned. Use the clothes you found on your bed." She turned away, not caring to argue the subject. I dressed. Everything felt stiff and scratchy, but had that fresh fabric smell that was pleasant but never lasted long. Arm came out of his room dressed exactly as I was. We looked at each other, both embarrassed.

"Maybe you geeve up the horses an' go work in the mercantile," Arm said. "You dress for it."

"Me? You look like that damned fool Dansworth did yesterday, 'cept fatter."

Arm made the gesture with his hand that was understood in all languages, and we went down to eat.

After breakfast and a smoke, I got the halter I'd brought in the night before. "I didn't want cold leather on the stud's face," I explained to Blanca.

"You need a wife," she said, "then you don't bother with no loco horse."

I got a bucket of grain and a flake of hay from the barn and when I got to the corral, Arm was already sitting on the top rail. I climbed up and over. The bay looked at me as I approached him, but there was no fire in his eyes. He was slowly becoming accustomed to me—and figuring out that I was the guy who fed him daily.

I tossed the hay at the snubbin' post and set down the grain bucket in front of me. Naturally, he was going to go for the grain first. As he dipped his head I held the halter in front of his muzzle an' he slid right into it. I closed the buckle and took a couple steps back.

The stallion stood there for a long moment, trying to figure out what the hell was going on. Then, he decided he didn't like whatever the thing was on his muzzle and behind his ears, and commenced to buck, squeal, rear, strike, and anything else he could think of. He even dropped to the ground and rubbed his head back and forth trying to get rid of the halter. I stepped back another few steps to be out of his range if he decided to kick my ass for me. He didn't.

"Now he gonna try to scrape it off with his good foot, like the *perro* scratching a flea," Arm called to me. I nodded. That's what ninety-nine out of a hundred horses would have done. The bay didn't, perhaps because he couldn't carry most of his weight on his twisted foot. Instead, he lowered his face into the grain bucket and began to chew. I walked over to where Arm was an' climbed up. "Tell the truth, I thought you were pooshing too fast with the halter this day," he said, slapping me on the back. "But I was wrong."

"I'm a little surprised myself," I said. We sat there and watched the stud empty the grain bucket and walk over to the hay. I found myself looking at the strange tracks he'd left in the inch of snow that'd fallen overnight. He tracked perfectly—rear hoof dropping precisely on top of the imprint in the snow made by the front hoof.

Armando must have seen where I was looking. "Ees too bad. With four hooves, the horse, he run the ass offa them thoroughbreds the reech people race. He beat the short horses, too."

"They're not called short horses no more," I said. "Now they're quarter horses."

"Well, hell. Same teeng."

We sat on the top rail for a time. I have to admit that watching a horse eat hay isn't what a fella would call exciting. "Wanna go fetch our mare?" I asked Arm.

"I got only a little money an' you 'mos busted, too. I'll get some from under the bed for both of us. Then we ride, no?"

I'll be the first to admit that keeping all that money under my bed wasn't the smartest thing we'd ever done. Still, we figured we'd often need quick access to it and neither of us trusted banks. Neither of the ladies would steal a sip of ice water in hell, so the money was safe where it was.

It's hard to remember how cold winter is when a man is in the midst of a West Texas summer. But, winter is a bitch, and it seems like the wind never stops. A bucket of milk left outside will freeze solid, troughs for animals constantly need ice broken in them, and firewood is consumed at an impossible rate to keep at least one part of a room warm, directly in front of the fireplace. Good, well-cared-for saddles creak and groan, well pumps freeze, making them impossible to use, and wind whistles through the best of houses—including ours.

We rode into Hulberton with scarves wrapped around our faces, bundled in herder's coats, and thick sheepskin gloves. Our horses grew beards almost immediately—the freezing of their moisture as they breathed out. Running a horse could—and probably would—burn his lungs because of his gulping of the arctic air.

And let me tell you this: there's nothing quite like a West Texas storm. Cattle on pasture huddle together and freeze solid, as dead as the statues they appear to be. A yard of snow isn't a big deal; some of the storms last three and four days and dump five feet or more of snow.

Farmers, ranchers, and settlers string ropes between their houses and barns. It's easy to get lost in the blinding white fury of a storm. Men and women freeze to death a few feet from their homes.

We rode up to Tiny's barn and tied our horses at the rail. They'd be fine; the cold wasn't a real ballbuster, and the wind was slowing down some.

Tiny had most of his sale horses in stalls and those outside clustered together at the edge of the barn, out of the wind. Tiny was graining the stalls as we shoved up the front sliding door wide enough to get in, and then closed it.

"Your mare is in the second stall from the end," Tiny said. "I got a pot of coffee going on my forge fire. Help your ownselfs—I'll be with you in a bit." Arm and I did just that, using metal cups that hung from horseshoe nails on the wall. It was no surprise that the coffee was half whiskey.

"Ees good," Arm said. "Warm a man's blood, no?"

We took our coffee down to the second-to-last stall and looked over our mare once again. She was as near to a perfectly conformed horse as I've ever seen. There was a gentleness in the depth of her chestnut eyes as she looked at us for a treat. Tiny had a bushel of crab apples against the wall. I got one and palmed it to the mare. She took it— gently—and crunched away at it.

"We done good," Arm said.

I pulled off a glove and reached into my pocket for Tiny's money. We watched the mare until Tiny was finished with his chore, and then the three of us walked back to the coffeepot. I handed our friend the cash.

"I got the bill of sale all wrote out," Tiny said. He took a neatly folded sheet of paper from the drawer of a small table and handed it to me. I didn't check it over any more than Tiny counted the cash I'd given him. That isn't the way we do things. A man's word is as good as he is, and Tiny was a good man. He poured himself a cup of coffee and topped off our cups.

"You gonna take her back today? She's welcome to stay here as long as you want," Tiny said.

"We got the hay an' grain already," Arm said. "We're ready for this fine mare."

"Dansworth was snooping around again yes-tiddy evening," Tiny said. "What he told me was that he was looking for a couple horses to save his trip from bein' a waste, but he spent most of his time lookin' at your mare."

"I guess that dude sumbitch can look all he wants, but he no gettin' near our mare," Arm said.

The sliding door began to open and all of our heads snapped in that direction. The two men who'd stopped at our ranch eased into the barn and shut the door behind him. They approached us.

Ignoring Tiny and Armando, one of them spoke directly to me. He reached into his pocket and pulled out a wad of bills. "This here's five hundred dollars," he said. "Mr. Dansworth wants that mare."

"Mr. Dansworth can go to hell," I said.

"What he wants, he gets," the man said. "He'll own that mare one way or another." He turned and he and his partner went to the front of the barn and out. They left the door open.

"You boys keep a close eye on that horse," Tiny said.

Chapter Five

We had a helluva storm a couple of days after we brought the mare to the ranch. Arm and I rigged a shelter for the mustang. He would have battered his way through a stall in five minutes—he'd never been in an enclosed structure before. The mare, our horses, and our packer we kept in stalls. We'd run a stout length of rope from our back door to the barn door—and we needed it. I also ran one from the house to the corral where the mustang was. I doubt if I'd have been able to find the barn or the corral, 'cept for sheer luck, without that guideline. Every year we hear about a man or woman freezing to death within a few yards of safety in their home or barn.

The wind howled like a devil hound from hell and the snow was whipped parallel to the ground, mounding into massive drifts against anything that attempted to challenge the power of the storm.

Teresa and Blanca didn't seem to be bothered by the storm. They had all the supplies they needed to feed us royally for at least a few weeks, and the safety of our horses was of no consequence to them—it was clearly defined man's work.

Armando and I had different perspectives on our weather-imposed captivity. We found a checkerboard on a bookshelf and it didn't take long to make little discs to use as men: mine were carrot coins and his were slices of pickle. We played several games, all of which I won. That pissed Arm off no small amount—he wasn't a man who could live with losing at anything.

His face was almost scarlet red and his hand trembled as he moved his pieces. "Arm," I said, "let's knock it off, okay? It's only a dumb game and you're gettin' all wound up 'bout it."

"Ees a gringo game, no? If we play a Mexican game, I keek your white ass."

"Maybe so. The thing is—they're only games. Ya know? I don't see why you get so bent an' twisted over a game. It's crazy."

"Now I am loco, no?"

I sighed. "Let's have a drink."

Arm's usual calm demeanor returned immediately. "Ees bes' idea you've had in a long time, Jake. You gotta learn to calm down, no?"

I fetched a bottle from the kitchen cupboard without responding.

Later—after we'd done some damage to our booze supply—Arm bundled up to check things out in the barn, muck the stalls, and feed hay and grain. I put on pretty near every piece of clothing I owned and followed the guide rope to the corral. Horses are herd animals by nature—they don't like being alone. I think that worked in my favor with our stud. I wasn't another horse, but I was better than no company at all.

I slung a ration of molasses oats over my back

and a flake of hay under my arm—I'd stashed a bale of hay and a supply of grain in our mud-room when the storm was still building—and went to visit our stallion.

It ain't like he greeted me with a smile and a song or as a long-lost brother, but he didn't offer to take me apart, either. The shelter we'd built, which was a simple triangle of barn wood with one open side, was holding up well. Snow was drifted against the windward side, which actually kept some of the horse's natural heat inside with him.

I fed him his grain and broke up the flake of hay in front of him. He dove into the grain and began to nibble hay. I reached very, very slowly for his face when he raised his head to chew. He'd built up quite a beard of frozen spittle and exhalation, and I figured it couldn't be any too comfortable for him. He took a half step back, but then stood. Moving as slowly as I possibly could I reached out my right hand and busted off a good part of the icicle. The bay's eyes widened for a moment and his muscles tensed. I was set to leap to the side if he lunged at me. We stared into each other's eyes for what seemed like a long time and then the horse dropped his head and went back to his hay.

What the hell, I thought. In for a penny, in for a dollar. I touched his shoulder very gently. He tensed up all over again, staring at me with a long stem of hay hanging from his mouth. We watched each other again for a bit and he went back to his hay and I kept my hand on his shoulder.

Some of the best trainers and horsemen I know mumble to their horses, not necessarily making any sense, but making human sounds. Some sing—Christmas carols, sea songs, bawdy stuff, whatever—but it's all done in a droning sort of monotone. I decided not to push my luck.

There were lots of horse apples behind the bay, but I didn't dare fork them out. I moved a good amount of them with my boot so he wouldn't be standing in them. I'd have loved to take a hoof pick to his feet, but anything like that would be a long time coming. I broke up the ice in the small water trough in his shelter and left him with his hay. I felt real good about how it'd gone.

I followed the line I'd rigged from the corral to the barn to help Arm with the chores, but he was almost finished with his work there. He had the mare out in cross ties in the midaisle between the lines of stalls, and was checking her hooves.

He was at her right rear. "Look," he said. He tapped the mare's hock and she immediately raised her hoof up to be examined. Arm straddled it and cleaned the manure out of it with a hoof knife. "This gal, she had real good care an' training, too. I peek up all her feet jus' as easy as this one."

I looked over my horse, Arm's, and the packers. Arm had mucked the stalls, cast a few handfuls of lime on the floor, and put down lots of fresh straw. The water buckets were filled and each animal had a ration of hay. "I don' give molasses grain today—eet gives them too much desire to run, no?"

"Good idea. We don't know how long the storm's

gonna last. Seems like the sumbitch has already gone on forever."

"Es muy verdad."

We followed the guideline to the house. Arm was in front of me by maybe a yard, and I couldn't see him at all. It seemed to me that the storm was becoming stronger and the snow thicker, rather than abating.

Once in the house holding mugs of half coffee and half booze, Arm suggested another game of checkers. I declined. "I don't feel like arguing with you, my friend. You're too much of a *pendejo*—making up your own rules and pissing vinegar every time you lose—which is every game we play."

We sat at the kitchen table. Armando grumbled a bit about the checkers, but then we began to talk about both our favorite topics—horses, and particularly, our horses—the mare and the stallion.

"Theese is not the best time to breed," Armando said. "It ain't the natural time, you know? If we cannot bring mare into heat, our stud will do her no good."

"Yeah. But even during the winter, the cycle is about twenty to twenty-five days. If we can tease hell outta her with the bay, an' then breed, we could catch her at the right time."

"Sí. But eleven months later—een winter again—we have a foal."

"Well, hell. That gives us plenty of time to insulate a birthing stall an' a stall for the mare an' foal to wait out the rest of the winter in."

"Eensulate?"

"Yeah. Double-board it covering cracks, hang

thick blankets to keep out chill, maybe—if we need to—cut a barrel in half an' get a small fire goin' in it. Anyway, we got nothing to lose by trying, right?"

"*Sí*. If the stud, he is a good breeder, we keep him on her two, three times a day. Then, if she gonna take, she weel."

"She'll take, okay," I said. "An' once she's in foal we can search out some more horses."

Armando sighed, sipped at his coffee, and then said, "Ees a long time to get this operation goin'."

"You got somethin' better to do, partner?"

"Sheet. Always with the smart-ass answer you are."

We went to bed that night and in the morning the storm was gone, only the hugely mounded drifts of snow letting us know it had made us prisoners for a few days. That's the way the West Texas weather runs. A storm will blow like hell for a couple, three, maybe four days, then it'll be gone as suddenly as it hit.

After our usual overly large breakfast, we decided to ride into Hulberton and visit with Tiny. There was nothing we really needed, but we were both stir-crazy. As it turned out, our horses were as anxious to get out as we were. We saddled up in the barn, led them out, and climbed on them. We had a short rodeo then: both horses bucked, twisted, snorted, and tried to get under the bit. We laughed an' slapped the silly sonsabitches with our hats, letting them burn off some boredom and energy.

There was a couple of feet of snow all over, and, like I said, massive drifts here and there. Traveling in snow tires a horse—there's a drag on the feet and legs—but ours were so fired up at being outside that they kept on attempting to run. After a few miles they calmed down some and behaved themselves.

We heard Tiny's hammer striking his anvil way the hell out from town, just as we almost always did. The sound was good and clean and bell-like, and for whatever reason, it seemed to lift from us the weight of the boredom the storm had generated. We let our horses pick up their pace regardless of the snow.

Tiny had a bucket of beer next to his forge, but there was precious little left in it. "Why I do this shit, I dunno," he said, holding up a piece of an ornamental door latch he was making.

"You get paid good for it, no?" Arm said.

"A whole lot more than it's worth," Tiny said. "Anyway, have some beer."

"There isn't enough left there to give a flea a footbath," I pointed out.

"Not in that bucket—but the one sitting in the snowbank outside is full."

I went back out, saw the bucket, and carried it in. We each had a couple of coffee mugs full while Tiny's craftswork cooled. "I got somethin' real fancy to show you fellas," Tiny said. "Come on back."

He led us to one of the rear stalls. In it an Appaloosa colt—maybe five or six months old—stood on spindly-looking legs, his eyes open wide, looking at us not with fear, but out of curiosity. "He's a strange one," Tiny said. "He ain't been weaned much more'n a month or so, or 'least that's what the fella sold him to me said. He said the mare got a twisted gut an' croaked. He—the colt, I mean—ain't stole. I got good papers on him."

Arm and I stood at the stall gate looking the little guy over. He was near the prettiest thing I ever saw—but I guess I'd say the same thing about just any colt or filly. Arm leaned over the gate. The colt moved a couple of steps to him and put his muzzle up to Arm's face. Arm breathed into the little guy's nostrils for a minute or so before the colt stepped back.

"How much you want for him?" Armando asked, already hauling money out of his pocket. Tiny laughed. "I figure you'd want him. Lookit the color—them splotches an' spots of black against his gray, well a man jist don't see too often."

"Havin' a young 'un around can help bring a mare into heat, even if it ain't hers," I said. "Have you had a halter on him yet?"

"The fella sold him to me had a rope halter on him an' was leadin' him like a packhorse. He's been handled a lot, too. You can tell that right off. You seen how he interduced hisself to Arm."

"Why'd the owner sell off such a fine colt?" I asked.

"He was a farmer—I seen him a couple times in the saloon. He said farmin' ain't nothin' but sweat, debt, an' disappointment an' he was sellin' his place an' everything on it an' goin' to Chicago to live with his brother—gonna work in his brother's store, is what he said."

"Well, I'll tell ya, Tiny," I said. "This boy, he's

goin' home with us if we have to tie you up an' steal him."

"It'd take more'n you two pissants to do that," Tiny laughed. "I gotta get forty-five dollars an' a trip over to the saloon. Hell, I gave almost that much for him."

"Boolsheet. Still, is a good price." He handed some bills to Tiny. "You ready for that trip 'cross the street?"

The saloon was, as usual, murky, with dingy clouds of tobacco smoke and the stink of stale beer and spilled whiskey and blood permeating it. It took a few seconds for my eyes to adjust. When they did I noticed that the two riders who'd been at our place before the storm were standing at the bar, along with a half dozen cronies just as low-down and dirty as they were. The original two moved out from the bar and both started flapping their gums to the others. Finally, the largest of them walked over to us. He wore his gun low and he had the shiny, oily-appearing eyes that indicate that a man enjoys inflicting pain. He stood facing the three of us.

"Pancho," he said, "I heard you an' your little friend threw a couple of my boys lookin' for work off your land, an' didn't even offer a cup of coffee to them."

"My name is no Pancho," Arm said. "An' that trash wasn't lookin' for no jobs."

"My name ain't Pancho neither—an' I'll stick by what my pard just said."

Tiny said, "Bring the rest of your litter-mates over here. We'll take the whole damned bunch of you on. Otherwise, shut the hell up."

Tiny was standing in the middle, between Arm an' me. "I ain't armed," he said. "But if you slugs want to trade punches, let's have at it."

"You got it all wrong," the big fella said. "Me an' the boys is jist out here tryin' to buy some horses for Mr. Dansworth." He smiled, showing he was missing several front teeth and that the ones he did have were yellow-gray and leaned in all different occasions. He put his right hand out to shake with Tiny. Out of instinct, I guess, Tiny extended his hand. Then the big guy clobbered Tiny with a sucker punch left to the mouth that snapped Tiny's head back. That was a signal to the men at the bar to join in an' have some fun kicking our asses. I grabbed up a chair an' busted it over the head of one of the rushing bunch. Tiny drove his right fist into the big man's gut and caught his nose and mouth with his knee as the big fella doubled over.

Arm attacked the two who'd been at our ranch, getting between them and then slamming their heads together. The sound was like that of a melon being dropped to a hard floor from about six feet up.

Tiny picked up the big man like he were a sack of grain and pitched him into the crowd of his cohorts. I was using a leg from the chair I busted, swinging it like a club. I connected real solidly with one fella's chin and he went right on down. Arm threw himself at an opponent, carried him to the floor, sat on his chest, and purely whacked hell outta the guy's face. The big man was struggling to his feet. Tiny walloped him again with a roundhouse right to the chin and that boy was out of the fight. Arm left the one on the floor unconscious and traded blows with another. He also kicked the new opponent squarely in the balls, dropping him clutching his groin, his scream more feminine than masculine. The couple that were left standing backed off in a hurry. The three of us went to a table and sat. I'd kind of wondered why no guns were pulled until I saw the tender sweeping a sawed-off twelve gauge at the melee. "You boys want your regular set up?" he called to us. I nodded and told him to make everything double.

Dansworth's men were dragging their wounded to the rear of the bar. I drew my .45 and put it on the table and Arm did the same.

"No need for the iron, boys," the bartender told us. "Any one of those assholes grabs a pistol and him an' anybody near him goes down with a bellyful of double-ought shot."

We relaxed with our beers and whiskeys after the tender brought his tray over. "Them saddlebums been lookin' for trouble all day," he said. "I guess they found some. Ain't my job to sort out my customers, an' as long as they were payin', I was pourin'. But when I see you boys walk in, I knew there was gonna be some grab-ass. They been talkin' a awful lot 'bout a buckskin mare you got from Tiny that Dansworth wants pretty bad."

"I guess they don' know what 'no for sale' means."

"I'll tell you this," the tender said. "Don't think Dansworth doesn't have some real tough boys—gunfighters—on his payroll. These turds you punched around are his scrub-work losers. You watch yourselves an' your horse."

I nodded an' said, "Thanks—we'll keep our eyes open."

He started back to the bar, stopped, and looked at me. "You owe me for a perfectly good chair, Jake."

I put a bill on the table.

We spent another hour in the saloon and then went back to Tiny's shop. He fit a halter—a nice one, leather, not rope—over the Appy's snout. That little colt followed us like a boy's puppy follows him to school.

When we got back to the ranch our mare was gone.

Arm and I stood at the open stall door as if in shock.

"Won' be hard to track weeth the snow. We take some jerky an' set out, no?"

"Yeah. But how could someone be stupid enough to steal a horse when a blind man could track up? I think we're bein' set up for an ambush—an' once we're dead, Dansworth will have the mare without having to worry about us taking her back or even goin' to the law."

"These rustlers, they would no go toward town. We know that much. We leave now, ride at night, catch up, fight rustlers, get our mare back, no?"

"Looks like that's the only choice we have, Arm."

We put the colt in a stall with hay, grain, and water, filled our saddlebags with jerky, and a bottle of half coffee, half whiskey, and moved out.

The trip from Hulberton to the ranch was a slow one because of the colt, so our horses weren't fatigued—they were as ready as we were.

The tracks told us there were four men and that one of them, riding a bit to the side, was leading the mare. Nothing indicated that there were outriders with a plan to somehow catch us in the middle from cover and shoot hell outta us.

Darkness fell quickly but there was a three-quarter moon and no cloud cover. The prairie was easily light enough to follow the tracks. We kept our speed down but we covered ground well.

After a couple of hours of riding we reined in and loosened our saddles to let our horses blow.

"This ees too easy," Arm said, after a long drink from our bottle. "It don' make no sense."

"I've been thinking the same thing," I said. "We gotta split up, Arm. Come at these men from two sides 'stead of riding square into an ambush."

Arm scuffed at a hoofprint in the snow. "We are getting closer to them," he said. "Look, see how clean these track is? It ain't a hour old—maybe a lot less."

"You have plenty of ammo, right?"

"Sí."

"Me, too. Good. How about you swing out left and I'll go out right?"

Arm was quiet for a moment. "Not far ahead—a few miles, maybe—there's a bunch of outcroppings, no? Ees excellent cover. I was ridin' one day an' came upon them."

"Sounds like where they might try to take us out," I said. "Let's ride out wide an' then close in.

If we're wrong, it won't take a minute to pick up the tracks again."

I went out about three quarters of a mile and then picked up the direction in which Arm and I were originally headed. The outcroppings my partner had spoken of were new to me; I hadn't done nearly as much exploring as he had. But, with the natural light, I didn't think I'd have too much trouble finding the spot. Even so, I rode past the rocks and had to look back over my shoulder to make certain I was seeing what I was looking for. The snort of a horse told me I was past where I'd planned to be—but that offered me a hell of an advantage.

I ground-tied my horse and eased my rifle out of the saddle scabbard. I jacked a round into the chamber and then began walking very slowly back toward the rocks and boulders.

I figured Arm would be coming in from the side, and I didn't care to have him plug me, assuming I, too, was moving in from the side I'd taken. I got close enough to where I could hear conversation and some laughter and fired a shot into the air. "You're surrounded!" I bellowed. "Mount up and ride out and leave the mare right where she is and you won't die!"

Arm immediately picked up on the "surrounded" bit and fired a couple of rounds, one of which hit a rock and sang its ricochet whine. I couldn't see the outlines of the men or the horses and I was afraid to shoot at where I thought the rustlers would be; I could easily plug our foundation mare. My partner didn't seem to have the same problem. He fired again and I heard the unmistakable sound of a bullet striking flesh and then a long, gurgling moan.

A barrage of lead erupted from the rocks. Nothing came close to me and each shot gave me a target: a muzzle flash. I shot, apparently took down a man from the scream I heard, and then I rolled like hell to avoid giving the rustlers the same advantage they'd so kindly given me.

Armando was shooting fast—the reports of his 30.30 were constant. He was on the other side of the outcropping, so I couldn't see his muzzle flashes. A slug hit a foot from me and I cranked several rounds at the bright light of the rustler's rifle. He yelled in pain and then was quiet.

The shooting stopped and the silence seemed louder than the battle had. "Anybody alive in there drop your weapon an' walk out with hands up!" Arm shouted. Nothing happened. I stood— still crouched a bit—and began walking toward the outcropping. It was possible we'd gunned all four men—but it was also possible one or two were playing possum on us.

Arm reached them before I did and shouted, "There's four down here, Jake. Looks like the horses are up ahead fifty yards or so. I count five horses—our mare is okay."

We both advanced to the cluster of what we thought were dead or dying rustlers. As it turned out, we were wrong. One man, splayed on the ground, jerked around and lowered a pistol at me. I'd kept a round in the chamber and so had Arm. We fired together and both hit the man—he didn't have a chance. Another of them moaned. Arm shot him and I saw the fellow's head jerk up and drop back down. A large piece of his skull skittered off into the prairie.

"Thass it," Arm said. "Les' get our mare an' go home."

We took the saddles off the rustlers' horses and dumped them right there—they were cheap Mexican junk. The horses weren't much better: all were far underweight and the breathing of a couple of them sounded like they had gravel in their lungs. We removed their bits and slapped them on their rumps. They'd find a bunch of mustangs to run with before long. Our mare was standing calmly, eyeing us, a too-tight rope halter over her head and muzzle. I loosened the halter and used the outlaw's lead rope to bring her with me to where I'd left my horse. She followed me with no problem. I took a wrap around my saddle horn with the rope and was mounting when Arm rode up. He must have left his horse closer than I did mine. I could see the whiteness of his teeth in a broad smile as he approached. "We done good, no?" he called.

I swung into my saddle. "Yeah, Arm, we done good. You got that bottle of booze an' coffee?"

"Was left of eet, anyway. I had a snort or *dos*." He handed me the bottle. I drank the couple of inches that remained in it and tossed it toward the dead rustlers. It smashed against a rock and the pieces glittered in the moonlight.

We headed for home, the mare following nicely.

We rode side by side, close enough to each other to talk in a normal tone of voice. Nevertheless, it was some time before any words were exchanged.

"Them stars up there," Arm said, "were right there when we killed the rustlers, no?"

"Sure. Far as I know, stars don't change no matter what goes on down here."

"Thass the thing. When a man's life, it is ended, nothing changes—nothing big, anyway."

"Maybe it depends on the man who dies. The way I see it, those rustlers needed to be shot an' killed. But, if you died, well, I'd be awful busted up about it. See what I mean?"

"No. Could be the rustlers, they had families or somethin'."

"Could be," I agreed. "But the fact remains that they was stealin' our horse."

Armando was quiet for some long moments. I looked up at the stars again and was doing so when he asked, "How many men you kill, Jake?"

"I dunno. Maybe ten, twelve—I dunno."

"I don' know how many I keel, either. More'n twelve, I think." He waited a bit. "It ain't right, Jake. Maybe with this Busted Thumb Horse Ranch we will no longer keel men, no?"

"Maybe not."

"Be good if we keel no longer."

"I s'pose it would, Arm. But to tell the truth, I can't see it happening that way."

"*Sí.* Sounds nice, though."

Arm had picked up a pack of playing cards on his last trip to the mercantile. Neither of us were big on gambling, but we decided we could play "21" for matchsticks. The first time Blanca came through the kitchen as we sat holding cards, she swept the deck from the table, jerked the cards out of our hands, gathered up the whole mess, and tossed it in the trash. She hollered at us in Spanish, which Arm later translated for me. "Cards," she said, "are tickets to hell! Satan loves to see men holding them because then he knows that those men will roast and scream in the eternal fire for all eternity. Teresa and me will not stay in a house where cards are played!"

That ended our pastime quite effectively. If we had to go back to our own cooking, we'd probably rather be in hell.

Winter drags on forever in West Texas. The sun we cursed during the summer rarely showed its face, and each day was a gray, dreary, and arctically cold repeat of the one that came before it, interspersed with storms.

I spent lots of time with the bay stallion. I'd let him off the rope holding him to the snubbing post and he danced and bucked and carried on like a colt at his freedom. He still often skittered away when I approached him. On good days, though, he'd follow me a step behind as I carried out his grain and hay. Nevertheless, any loud, unexpected noise scared hell out of him. A heap of snow sliding down from the barn's roof with a long *whoooosh* frightened him, so he took off in his awkward run and damned near slammed into the corral fence. Then he turned, nostrils flared, pawing the ground in front of him, challenging the sound. It took him a full day to come down from that little episode.

The thing is, there's always noise around a working ranch. Arm and I talked it over and decided that on an irregular schedule, we'd clatter pots an' pans or fire our rifles or pistols, or yell as loud as we could at least once a day. That was tough on the stud. His nature told him to either fight or haul ass when something threatened him. For a few days he ate his grain and drank water but left his hay to blow around in the corral. It took about ten days to bring him to a point where he'd tighten at a strange sound, but wouldn't bolt or rear.

The mare was getting prettier by the day. I swear if she were a woman, I'd have married her. The Appy was growing out of coltishness and beginning to grow into a horse. He put some muscle on his legs, his chest broadened and filled out, and his ass went from lean slabs of muscle to the semirounded rump we were looking for. He had a hell of a personality, too. Armando was his obvious favorite since Arm fed and brushed him daily, but he tolerated me, usually poking his snout at me for a treat. The packer was getting fat and we probably should have sold him off since we didn't see any future use for him, but we both liked him, and we could easily afford to feed him, so we kept him and let him grow fatter. He seemed to appreciate our generosity.

Going into Hulberton became a big treat to Arm and me. We'd drag Tiny away from his work—which didn't take a ton of effort—and suck beer in the saloon for a few hours. Then we'd ride back to the ranch feeling good an' at peace with the world.

There were still a crew of Dansworth men hanging around, but they wouldn't look us in the eye and they didn't seem to be causing any particular trouble—at least until the buffalo hunter with the Sharps came to town and began hanging with Dansworth's men.

We first noticed him when the three of us were drinking beer and talking about horses. He was a big man, like most shaggy hunters, tall and heavy with muscle rather than fat. He was long-bearded and his hair hadn't seen scissors in a long time. He wore leggings and a greatcoat, both made from buffalo hides. He sat with his back to the wall, a bottle and a glass in front of him, and a Sharps rifle across his lap.

Christian Sharps was a bookish kind of guy who held the patent on the most deadly sniper weapon used in the War of Northern Aggression. He operated out of Hartford, Connecticut, and didn't turn out a lot of his rifles, but the ones he made and sold were perfect. They fired a .52 slug that could pass through a horse, a man, and still have the power to kill another man. It literally tore arms and legs off if the shot struck a limb rather than the body mass. Anyone who took a .52 slug from a Sharps in the body was dead.

"There's trouble, no?" Arm said, eyeing the man.

"Yeah," I said. "For sure."

Tiny glanced over. "He looks hard," he said, "but that buffalo gun don't mean nothin' less he knows how to use it. It's as easy to miss with a Sharps as it is with any rifle. Hell, I got a Sharps breechloader my uncle left to me when he croaked. I tried her out a few times, but couldn't hit nothin' with her. I think the rear sight was bent a tad, an' maybe the front, too. An' I never did figure out that elevation sight. I didn't care 'nough about it to put no work into it fixin' the sights an' then firing her in until she shot true."

Arm and I stared at each other as if we'd been told that pigs sang songs an' nested in trees.

"You got a Sharps?" I asked.

"I jus' said I did, didn't I?"

"You weel sell us the rifle?" Arm asked.

"Hell, no. It ain't fit nor fair to sell somethin' a dead man left to you. I'll lend her to you, though. I got no use for it. I ain't big on guns, tell the truth. I don't carry one like you boys, an' I don't care to."

Tiny wanted to keep on drinking, but we goaded hell outta him to go to his place and get the rifle. Finally, after we bought a pair of buckets of beer to take out, he gave in.

The Sharps was in a hard case and was wrapped in deerskin. There was some light rust on the barrel, and there was a gouge in the stock where a bullet had hit it, but other than that it looked just fine. I put the butt to my shoulder and I could immediately see that both the front and rear sights had taken a beating, maybe when the rifle was dropped onto a hard surface. It didn't look like it'd take much to fix things and then run some bullets through the rifle to sight it in.

The clerk at the mercantile had to scrounge around in his storeroom to find any .52 ammunition, but he finally came up with three boxes of fifty each. He wanted six dollars for all of them. I gladly paid the exorbitant price.

We rode back to the ranch a little faster than we usually did—I was that keen on seeing what I

could do with that fine Sharps rifle. All I really
needed was a pair of pliers to straighten the two
sights. I ran a piece of cloth saturated with Hoppe's
gun oil through the barrel and carefully lubricated
the hammers and the two triggers this model had.
Arm stood next to me watching, shifting from foot
to foot, asking a question every so often. I wasn't a
rifle expert, but I'd picked up some knowledge
here and there. It was coming dark when I thought
the rifle was ready to be tested.

"Maybe we should wait until tomorrow," I said.

"Boolsheet."

We walked out through the snow a couple hundred yards from the house to a point where a
small stand of trees were a hundred or so yards
ahead of us. I slipped a slug into the breech and
brought the butt to my shoulder. It fit perfectly, as
if the weapon had been made 'specially for me. I
put the sights on a small tree and eased back the
first trigger and then moved my finger to the firing trigger. I took a breath and squeezed. The recoil knocked me on my ass, and the blaze of light
from the muzzle was as bright as lightning on a
dark night. I missed the tree—and as far as I
know, that slug is still traveling. Armando
laughed at me as I sat there in the snow, but then
there was a look of awe on his face as well. "*Jesús*,"
he whispered.

The thundering, percussive roar of the shot
rolled out and echoed back like that of a cannon.

The next morning we decided to go out on our
horses to test-fire the Sharps again. After all, it
was likely that the rifle would be used from
horseback or dismounted near the horses.

We rode beyond the stand of trees I'd shot at yesterday. There were no gauges or torn-away branches that'd show I'd hit anything. Armando made a couple of smart-ass remarks about my marksmanship, including, "Maybe you try to shoot the barn nex'? Is bigger than trees."

We'd fired pistols and rifles from the backs of our horses in the past, but there's no comparison to the sound those guns produced with the blast—the roar—of a Sharps. We each fired our pistols a couple of times and each squeezed off a few rounds of 30.30s from our rifles while mounted. Our horses were used to the sound by now and weren't bothered. We tied them well to a thick limb of an oak and walked a few yards away. There was a rock fifty yards away and even the weak and sullen sun made the bits of mica in the rock glint. It was a fine target.

I hunkered down to shoot from the standard sniper sitting position. The gun oil smelled fresh and good, and the furniture polish I'd used on the stock the night before gave off a sweet, woody scent. I leveled the Sharps over one knee, loaded a round into the breech, and took aim. I was steady and confident this time around. I squeezed the firing trigger, and this time my shoulder absorbed the recoil. A volcano of snow erupted a few feet to the left of the target. All that was fine. What wasn't fine was that both our horses were rearing, crazy-eyed, pulling against their reins, squealing in fright. We ran to them and, after a bit, were able to calm them without getting our heads smashed in.

It was Armando's turn to fire. He took the

same position I had, loaded up, and aimed for a long time. Finally, he fired. His round spurted snow into the sky almost on top of where my shot struck. That was good—I could adjust the sights again to come back to true from the left. What wasn't good was that our horses went berserk again, and it took us longer to calm them down.

"Ain' no other way to do eet," Arm said. "The silly sonsabitches gotta learn the Sharps, it won't hurt them no more than our pistols or 30.30s." Unfortunately, he was right, but I wasn't sure how much the animals could take. Both their mouths were bloody from yanking against the bit, both were trembling, and both had eyes as big as wagon wheels.

Arm stroked and calmed them as I took the pliers from my pocket and moved both the front and rear sights a frog's hair to the right. I looked back at Arm and the horses. He nodded that he was ready. I steadied myself, took the customary deep breath, and fired the Sharps. The rock didn't so much split or break as it did disintegrate, sending chips, pieces, and shards of sparkling mica-studded stone into the air as if it'd been shot into the sky by an artillery piece. It was an awesome and somewhat frightening sight. I couldn't help but visualize what would happen if a man were hit midbody.

Arm was standing between the two horses—which wasn't a good place to be—but he had control of their heads, his hands locked around the chinstraps that set the bit in their mouths. Their reaction to this round was less violent, but their trembling increased. "Shoo' again," Arm called.

I picked out another rock about 150 yards out. It was more of a boulder than a rock; with the Sharps now apparently sighted in, it'd be hard to miss. I jacked up the elevation bar a notch, took my stance, and fired. The thumb-size slug split the boulder like it was a loaf of bread cut with a sharp knife.

Arm nodded and yelled, "Go!"

I shot at the smaller piece of the boulder, spewing brownish dust and pieces of rock in all directions. "Ees 'nuff for today, Jake," Arm shouted. "Tomorrow we do another lesson, no?"

I checked over the horses' mouths. They were abraded by the bit rather than cut, and the blood and saliva mix had already ended. Both were skittish and on the edge of panic, but a good deal of stroking and talking to them eventually calmed them down.

On the way back we scared a jackrabbit out of a mess of dead brush—a common enough occurrence—but the horses reacted like barely sacked-out two-year-olds. We reined them in easily enough.

"Takes some time," Arm said.

I agreed. "They didn't do all that bad. We knew they'd come apart a bit when they heard the Sharps. I figure a couple more days and they'll settle on down."

"They will no like that rifle, but they'll live with it."

Back in the barn I spread udder balm on the bars of our horses' mouths—the part of the jawbone upon which the bit rests—and we rubbed them down, checked their feet, and fed them—adding an extra treat of molasses/oats mixture.

Arm had been unusually silent during all that process.

"What?" I said.

"We now have the beeg gun an' you can shoot the hairs offa fly's balls with it—but that fella in the saloon, he has the beeg gun, too. An' he shoots an' keels buffalo from far distance, no?"

"Yeah. But the thing is, he's shooting at an animal twice as large as a big bull, an' his target is standing still. When the shaggy hunters set up on a herd, they pick off those farthest from the center—and they're standing still, grazing. Shaggies are stupid, Arm. Hell, a shooter can drop one ten feet from another an' the other one will keep on grazing. That's the way those guys work a herd—start on the outside and shoot their way in. Hell, dropping twenty or thirty a day isn't rare."

"Es verdad?"

I nodded. "An' there's somethin' else, too. There's nobody shooting back at a buffalo hunter. That ain't the case with us."

We had a fairly moderate storm that started that afternoon. We left the horses in their stalls and Arm took the Sharps and went out into the wind and swirling snow a couple hundred yards and ran a half dozen slugs through the rifle.

Of course, the horses didn't like it, but they didn't come apart, either. They flinched each time Arm fired, and their eyes got a tad wide, but that was about the extent of their reactions.

Strangely enough, our packer raised his head

at the first shot and then went back to his hay, paying absolutely no attention to the other rounds. I left the barn and watched our stud in the corral. He snorted, ran a bit, and then pretty much clamed down. I suppose in his mind, the racket was a natural thing: thunder, maybe.

After all the barn and corral chores were done, Arm and I were damned near frozen. We went inside and shucked out of our heavy gear and sat at the kitchen table having a couple of slugs of whiskey and talking things over.

"Ees good—the Busted Thumb Horse Ranch," Arm said.

It's strange how rapidly things can change.

Chapter Six

A feeble storm swept in but it didn't have any balls to it—it was over in a couple of days. Nevertheless, both of us were stir-crazy and we decided that we should ride on in to Hulberton and visit Tiny. There was some wind when we started out, but it wasn't doing anything but shifting existing drifts around.

In town we sat in the saloon with ol' Tiny for a couple of hours or so. I noticed that a while after we came in, the buffalo hunter stood up, belched loudly, picked up his Sharps and left through the back door. Arm said he needed something from the mercantile, so he met Tiny and me back at Tiny's shop. Dusk was coming on and we didn't want to ride in the dark, so we made tracks out of Hulberton.

The wind was about the same as we left as it'd been when we came in—kind of annoying, but not threatening to dump another storm on us.

We left Hulberton at a jog and held that gait. The horses had been on vacation; they needed a little workout, lest they turn into butterballs as our packer had.

Arm had bought a pipe in town and a couple of

sacks of Green Mountain smoking tobacco. He was having a hell of a time keeping his new pipe lit, scratching stick match after stick match trying to suck the flame into his bowl. I rolled a smoke and lit it with a single match cupped in my hands. That kind of pissed ol' Arm off.

"Why such a goddamn hurry?" he snarled at me. "A man can no get a pipe . . ." He never finished the sentence. Instead his body was thrown violently to his right. He was hitting the ground as that unmistakable bellow of a Sharps reached us. I jumped down, told the horses to stay, and crouched over Armando.

His face was completely covered with red from his forehead to jaw, where blood was dripping steadily onto his coat. The blood sheeted downward and to the sides from a long gouge—like a shallow furrow—probably a good five inches long. I thumbed his neck pulse. It was thrumming nicely, steadily. I was surprised; I thought my partner of all those years was dead. I'll admit to the quick tears that ran from my eyes, and the huge lump that suddenly appeared in my throat, almost cutting off my breathing. I'll also admit to a fire of anger that flared in my belly as I snatched my Sharps from my saddle scabbard. It was already loaded—I carried it that way since it took two separate triggers to fire it.

Arm was mumbling curses as I brought the butt and made a sweep of the direction from which the shot must have come. The thought that if Arm had been a couple inches ahead of where he was, he'd be as dead as a lump of coal, and, more'n likely, his head woulda been torn off his shoulders. That flash of thought made the fire within me burn hotter and stronger.

I saw nothing on my first sweep. Then, on the second, I saw a drift that was covering a small cluster of rocks and boulders. I kept my sights there and ticked up the elevator ladder sight very slightly—the target was about 300 yards away. As I squinted into the thickening dusk, a gray horse's ass came into view. I'm not big on killing horses, but tht fire was almost out of control inside me. I put a round through the animal's spine and he dropped like a bucket down a well. I didn't like doing it, but I did it. That buffalo hunter tried to kill my partner and there was nothing I wouldn't do to take the sonofabitch permanently down and leave his corpse for the vultures.

I reloaded, keeping my eyes on the cover area. The day was ending and I wasn't about to let him run on back to Hulberton in the dark. He'd misgauged his shot or the wind or both. He wasn't as good as I was and I think we both knew that. I would have made the shot at Arm just as easily as I picked off the buffalo man's horse.

'Course my horse had scurried back a bit when I fired but I caught him up easily. I swung into my saddle and banged my heels against my horse's sides. He was ready to run. I jerked him from side to side in hard turns to make the moving target more difficult, should the buffalo man get lucky and draw a line on me. I felt hooves losing purchase on snow-covered ice a few times, but kept on asking for more speed.

The buffalo man tried a shot from behind his

cover. I heard that big slug whistle by a few feet to my right. As I raced up to the rocks I was pretty sure he'd try again. He did, and missed me by a lot. Then he began to run—clumsily, panicked, slipping and skidding in the snow. I grasped my reins in my teeth to free up my hands and shouted, "Hey!"

The damned fool turned toward me and I blew a hole the size of a cannonball in his chest. The impact threw him back like a rag doll hurled by a tantruming kid. I didn't ride up to see if he was dead. There was no doubt at all about that.

I rode back and fetched Arm's horse. Arm was still sitting on the ground. He'd wiped a good bit of the blood from his face and had his scarf tied around his head, pressing on his forehead. Without his hat he looked a Spanish pirate I remembered from a picture book I'd seen as a kid.

"You keel heem?" Arm asked as I reined in near where he sat.

"You betcha."

"*Bueno.* Back-shootin' sumbitch, he no deserve to leeve."

I didn't bother to point out that the buffalo man hadn't shot from anywhere near Arms's back. I figured a man who's just missed death by the slightest part of an inch deserves to say whatever he cares to.

I stepped down from my horse to help Arm onto his. He tried to push me away, cursing in Spanish, but I saw he was wobbly on his feet and that the places on his face where he'd cleaned away the blood were a sickly, pale white. He slumped a bit in his saddle, once he was mounted.

"Teresa and Blanca will doctor up that ditch in your forehead," I said.

"Boolsheet. I don' need no doctorin'. Ain't nothin' but a scratch, no?"

"No. It needs to be fixed a bit."

The Spanish cursing continued.

We rode back to the ranch at a walk and I noticed that Arm had both hands grasped on his saddle horn with his reins tied together just above his hands. It was full dark when we got back. I helped him off his horse and walked him into the house. I called the women down from their room and set them to work in fixing my partner.

Our horses—as well as the mare, the colt, and the stud—needed looking after an' I took care of all of them. The stallion actually hustled over to me when I climbed down into the corral with a bucket of grain and a flake of hay jammed under my arm.

The women had Arm stretched out on his bed on his back with a yellowish salve packed into his wound. Teresa was just wrapping a piece of cloth cut from a sheet around his head while Blanca held him steady as I walked into his room.

"Jake," Arm said, "these women, they will give me no tequila. You will fetch a bottle?"

I looked at Blanca. She shook her head negatively.

"Later on," I said.

"First, you will take a bowl of broth, then maybe a seep of tequila," Teresa said.

"Seep, my ass. I wan' the whole damn bottle."

"There is no need to talk like the campesino,"

Blanca said sternly. "We are not *putas*. You weel show a little respect, Armando."

"Damn leetle," Armando grumbled, not quite loud enough for the women to hear.

Teresa mixed a couple of pinches of a grayish powder into the bowl of beef soup for Arm and he slept quietly the entire night, without the tequila. In the morning he was as pleasant as a rattler in a bucket of boiling water. He tried to stand but fell back onto his bed. After another bowl of soup he slept the day away.

I talked with the women in the kitchen. "The powder, it makes for sleep an' healing. 'Fection is the only problem an' we don' see none of that. Lots of blood he lost, though. He needs the rest."

"Suppose he has a concussion or some such thing?" I asked.

"No 'cussion. None. His *ojos* are same," Teresa said.

"Equal, is what she means," Blanca said.

I went out to take care of the chores. After mucking out the stalls and cleaning the corral a bit, I fed the whole crew. I noticed that the colt had his nose in the air a good part of the time, and that the mare held her tail slightly raised from her rear end. I took a closer look and almost whooped with joy—I was pretty sure she was ready to be bred.

The problem was the stud—he was the big question. I didn't doubt that the mare would accept him, but I was concerned how he might damage her—some stallions get pretty rank, jamming their tool into the wrong orifice, or biting at a mare as he mounted her. If Arm was in better shape we could put ropes on the bay and wrestle him away from the mare if we needed to. But, he wasn't. The women, I'm afraid, would be useless—and there's the danger of catching a hoof in the head.

That left me two choices, and I needed to decide quickly since a mare stays in heat only a short time, particularly during winter. I could try it alone, or I could scramble into Hulberton and ask Tiny to come out and help me.

It didn't take long to make the decision or to saddle my horse and haul for town. On the way, I had some thoughts about the man I'd killed the day before. I felt no guilt or sorrow whatsoever—to me the shot I fired into him was of no more consequence than plugging a rabid coyote. I compared that with how I felt after Arm's gunfight with the kid and then decided there were simply no comparisons to be made, and put the whole matter outta my mind.

Tiny was enthusiastic about the breeding, and he had no work that day, anyway. He saddled up and we hustled back to the Busted Thumb. Tiny looked over the mare, noticed she was pissing frequently, saw the colt sniffing the air to catch her scent and revel in it, because that was all he was going to get to do, and then looked in on the stud. He, too, was spending a good deal of his time with his muzzle pointing upward, drawing in the scent of the mare.

We had Blanca tear off another piece of sheet. She grumbled, "All our sheets, they go to wounded men and *puta* horses."

Tiny wrapped the mare's tail near her genitals

to keep it out of the way. We decided to bring the mare to the stallion rather than attempting to bring the stud into the barn. We tied the mare outside the corral. She immediately began squealing and backing up to the fence. Tiny grinned. "This little lady is real ready," he said.

We opened the gate to the corral, dropped loops over the bay's neck and tied him to the snubbing post. It was more than clear that he was as ready as the mare; it looked like he'd grown a slightly shorter third hind leg.

As it turned out, I could have probably taken care of the breeding by myself. We led the mare into the corral, backed her to the stallion, and he climbed on as easily and smoothly as a dowager settling in a church pew. The deed itself took only a few minutes. Tiny was ready to guide the bay's tool if it slipped out, but it didn't. When it was obvious the deed was done we led the mare back to her stall in the barn.

We visited with Arm, who was still a tad woozy but becoming more alert, drank some whiskey, and then rode out to see if the buzzards had gotten to the buffalo man yet. They had. Six or eight were circling above and there was an equal number chowing down.

"I never had no use for them sonsabitches," Tiny said. "Hell, I'll take a deer when I need meat, but dropping shaggies from a half mile away and then tearing their hides off and leaving fifteen hundred or so pounds of good meat to rot jus' ain't right. I seen the results of a big stand once, an' it 'most made me puke. There must have been twenty buffalo on the ground and a crew was staking them out and making the cuts so that their mule team could drag off the hides. All that meat gone to waste . . ." He let the sentence die. We watched as one of the larger vultures dragged a length of pinkish white intestine from the corpse in its beak and flailed its six-foot wings at the others to keep them away while he ate.

We went back to the ranch and had lunch, a couple of tastes of whiskey, and then took the mare back to the stud. Both of them were still interested and went through the process again.

Tiny wanted to beat the dark to Hulberton and he rode off with my thanks. Maybe five minutes later he came back as I was unwrapping the mare's tail.

"You'd best keep a close eye on this gal," he said. "We had a audience when we was breedin'. I seen their tracks—it was three, maybe four men."

We'd been too busy to pay much attention to anything but the mare and the stud during the mating. I vowed I'd keep a close watch on our buckskin mare. I supposed I could have bundled up and slept out in the barn by the mare's stall, but it was cold enough to wreck a brass monkey, and I'd gotten right used to sleepin' in a real bed the past few months. I thought—very briefly—of bringing the mare into the mudroom at night. Then, I realized what Teresa an' Blanca would have to say about that. Hell, if I'd done it, we'd probably have mare stew for supper the next dinner.

Instead, I leaned some planks on the inside of the stall door and strung some tin cans—hoof ointment, udder balm, canned peaches, and so forth across the inside, just above the planks. It wasn't a perfect alarm system, but it was better than nothing, and I figured the noise would wake me up.

Arm came down for breakfast the next morning lookin' pretty good, except for the cloth wrapped around head. He ate with his usual voracious appetite. As he crammed his face I filled him in on the breeding and the tracks Tiny had seen.

"Tiny," Arm said, "he can make a bell quick as can be, no? We get one an' hang it on the stall door an' there ya go."

It was a good idea.

"We ride when I feenesh grub," Arm said, "get the bell today."

"Your ass we ride. You're not ready for it. Ride your bed today an' maybe tomorrow . . ."

"*Mañana?* Boolsheet."

We took it easy making the ride and Arm didn't seem to suffer any ill effects. We scouted out the spot where Tiny had seen the hoofprints in the snow and followed them into town, where they were quickly lost in the ruts and the mass of other tracks. There was no surprise there—we knew where they'd lead us. Tiny said he could bang out a bell with no trouble. "It'll have the tone like I made it outta a lump of soap—'cept it'll be loud. I've made these things before. I just gotta nail some shoes on that gray over there, an' I'll whack out your bell."

"*Bueno.* We wait in the saloon."

The bartender looked at us strangely as we

walked in and said, "Where's Tiny? He ain't gave up drinkin', has he?"

"No," I laughed. "He'll be right over."

"Whew," the tender said. "The last time he give it up my profits went to hell."

Arm and I had just about sat down when Dansworth walked over to our table. Even his gait showed his anger—he was stiff-legged and his heels struck the floor hard. His face was flushed and both his hands were clenched in fists. "I lost a good man yesterday," he said.

"Well, I'll tell you what. If we see him, we'll tell him you're lookin' for him," I said.

"Nex' time, hire on a gringo who can shoot," Arm said. "Maybe like Jake, here. You lookin' for ambush work, *mi amigo*?"

Dansworth worth reached into his suitcoat pocket. "You pull that Derringer and I'll kill you right where you stand," I said. There was a rapping sound from under the table. "This .45 is pointed at your chest, Dansworth. The table won't even slow the slug down."

Dansworth removed his hand from his pocket, empty. "I hear you covered that buckskin mare with a good-looking mustang a couple times, he said, his voice quivering with anger. "She might throw a good foal. But I'll tell you this: either the mare or the mare and the foal are going to be mine before I leave Hulberton."

I looked at Arm.

He said, "Boolsheet."

Dansworth sputtered a bit, little bits of spit escaping from between his lips. He spun on his heel and stomped back to where his cronies and flunkies sat at the rear of the saloon. "Nice visitin' with you," I called after him. "You might want to send one of your scum out to pick up what's left of your buffalo man. Ain't much left by now, but maybe you could bury him in a cigar box."

I slid my pistol back into my holster. Arm did the same; his .45 had been resting on his lap, muzzle pointed at Dansworth. "Seems he no like us much," Arm said.

"Hard to figure," I said, "nice fellas like us."

Tiny walked into the gin mill a half hour later, carrying what looked like a gallon-size bucket with a slight upward turn around its open end. There was a curl of steel to attach a rope to at the top.

"The theeng is," Arm said as he waved to the tender for Tiny's drinks, "suppose the rope is cut. Then the bell do nothing, no?"

"Yeah," Tiny answered. "That's why I made it so you can bang together a little rectangle of wood on the stall gate and nail the bell to it. Thataway, anyone screwing 'round with it is going to make noise."

"How loud is this thing?" I asked.

Tiny banged the clapper against the body of the bell. The tone was unmelodic, but it was loud. He grinned. "You boys will hear that, I'm wagerin'."

"Yeah, we will," I said. "If it gets us through the winter, we can set up a bunk for one of us to sleep on as the mare comes closer to birthin'."

"I was wonderin' about the stud," Tiny said. "Any chance Dansworth will try to steal him?"

"I'd dearly love to see him try. That horse barely

tolerates me, an' anyone else he'd stomp into the ground. He's his own alarm system."

"Damn. I had the thought of makin' up a shoe for that screwfoot—lift it up a bit and level it to the ground. But unless we tied and threw him, there's no way I could work on the foot."

"Even then you'd have a bushel of trouble, Tiny," I said. "And, hell, he's gotten around on that foot jist the way it is for a few years. I'd just as soon let it be."

We left within an hour, Arm and I both hot to build the little rectangle and attach it to the stall gate. Tiny refused money for the bell. I stuffed a bill into his pocket.

Our carpentry ain't much, but we didn't need much skill. The rectangle was a foot deep and attached to the stall gate with large nails. We banged the bell into place and swung open the gate. Tiny was right—it was pretty loud. "I'll go on up to my room an' you open an' close the gate," I said, "an' see how much sound reaches me."

I sat on my bed. The thunking of the bell would have awakened me, I'm sure of that. Since both Arm's and my rooms faced the barn, I was sure the alarm would raise my partner, too. I went back out.

"Theese I don' like much," Arm said. He unlatched the stall gate and opened it very slowly. There was barely a sound from the bell.

"They gotta get in the barn, open the gate, get a halter on the mare, an' lead her on out to wherever they're takin' her," I said. "That alone would wake us up. They gotta have at least two men—maybe three. There'll be some noise. I'm gonna sleep with the Sharps loaded up an' leanin' right next to my window."

"I do same with my rifle, Jake. Ain' nobody gonna steal our mare."

The next day, the mare refused the stud, dropping her head to kick at him, and twisting and turning to get away. For his part, the bay didn't seem overly interested, either. "She took good, no?" Arm smiled. "Now all we do is wait 'leven months an' we see what we get. Ees funny—a woman can make a baby in nine months, but a horse, she need eleven."

Winter lasts forever in West Texas. Arm and I did our chores and I continued working with the stallion, trying to get some of the shyness and aggressiveness out of him. I had no real reason to do that except that I liked the horse—he'd certainly never be a riding or ranch horse because of his warped foot.

The mare was a low-care animal. She was affable—sweet, even—and she never gave anyone any trouble. Even Teresa and Blanca would come out to the barn every so often and give the mare a treat, scratch her muzzle, stroke her neck.

The colt was a good horse, too. He was going to grow into something pretty large; his chest and the length of his legs showed that.

We were pretty sure the mare had taken. On a clear day we led her out to the corral and brought her in with the stud. He paid little attention and she was even less interested. Obviously, she was out of her heat cycle, but having the colt and the stallion around didn't arouse any interest on her part. We took that to mean that she was pregnant, but it was really far too early to tell.

I put some time in with the Sharps and became right handy with it. I got to the point where I could fire it from my horse's back, too. Arm went out target shooting with me every so often, but didn't have a ton of interest in the buffalo gun. "The 30.30, it does what I want it to do," he said. "I don't need no cannon."

We bought a little carriage for the ladies for Christmas and bought a trained horse—a nice bay that had some age on her—from Tiny to pull it. Blanca had mentioned how much they missed going to Mass on Sundays and holy days. They both learned to drive quickly and every Sunday they rolled out to Hulberton in their best clothes, and a buffalo robe covering their laps.

"The church, it is important to them," Arm said. "The surrey is good. It ain't like we can't afford to feed that ol' hoss."

It was coming spring when we began discovering more tracks around our place. The hoofprints didn't come terribly close to the house, barn, or corral, but they were within seeing distance. I wasn't surprised by the visitors. Dansworth was used to getting what he wanted in any manner he had to, and it was real clear he wanted the mare and probably the stallion, as well. Meanwhile, the damned fool was paying a dozen men or more to hang around the saloon, drink, play poker, grab an occasional whore, and to be available.

The mare had the slightest curve to her belly and Arm and I would have bet that she was pregnant. I don't think that curve got by Dansworth's men.

"You know," Arm said one morning as we stood outside the barn, smoking, "Dansworth can do theese one of two ways: he can attack with his men and keel us, or he can steal out the horses."

"I think I'd go with the attack—he not only wants our horses but he's pissed off at us enough to want to see us dead."

"We need some supplies, then, no? To make us an' the women safe?"

"Yeah—a ton of ammunition, a couple more rifles that we can post by the windows and in the barn, and whatever Teresa and Blanca want."

"Ees early yet," Arm said. "Might jus' as well go today, no?"

That's what we did. We decided to take the packer along, because the ladies needed sacks of flour, coffee, and sugar. "Sumbitch!" Arm cursed as he strapped the rig on the packhorse. "Theese boy almos' too fat for the rig. He is a *gordo*—eat allatime an' do nothin'."

"Well, why not give the ladies money when they go to the church, an' let them haul what they need? Ya know? They got their surrey and all we got is a lard-assed packer."

Arm agreed immediately.

That's the way it went. I handed over sixty dollars for whatever they needed to Teresa an' Blanca an' sent them on their way that Sunday morning. The extra rifles and ammunition would be tabbed by the mercantile owner and we'd pay him next time in town.

We stood outside the barn watching the surrey pull away, the women bundled in their heavy clothes, the big buffalo robe covering both their laps. There hadn't been much snow lately, but there'd been lots of wind. There were some bare spots on our land an' on the road to town. "Winter is 'bout over," I said.

"No it ain't," Arm said. "We ain't had the beeg one yet—the storm that people, they talk 'bout for years after. Nossir, winter is no over."

It turned out Arm was right.

But, the storm hadn't caused all the bloodshed and dead men.

You see, Blanca and Teresa set off for Mass that Sunday morning, and by afternoon, they hadn't come back.

"We can follow the tracks, no? Theese is too goddamn long they be gone."

It was about then that one of Dansworth's boys rode in. I recognized him, although I never knew his name. I saw him kill a man in a saloon in Laredo with a knife he pulled from his boot—sliced the poor guy's throat—and then walk outside and draw on the sheriff—kill him, and drop the law's deputy, as well.

He was awful handy and awful quick with his Colt. The sheriff of Laredo wasn't half bad, but he wasn't a gunfighter. The deputy couldn't outdraw a goat.

The gunman got on his horse—although there were lots of men who wanted to put a bullet into him. He hauled ass out of town before I had a chance to face him.

I was one of the men who thought he should be dead.

Killing like he did ain't nowhere right—'specially the deputy. He was maybe twenty years old, a towhead, whose badge was polished so much he musta worked on it every night.

The killer had a wolflike face—one I'll never forget. His eyes were set closely together in a narrow forehead and his nose and mouth stood out a bit, like the muzzle of a dog or a wolf.

The gunslinger rode up to our barn and dismounted. He stood there holding his reins, letting us walk from the house to him. His horse was a nice-looking black mare with a blaze on her face, but she needed some weight, and their were spur marks on her flanks. A large Mexican bit—what's called a "spade bit," which is a cruel bit of tack—was buckled too tight over her muzzle.

"I'm here to pick up a buckskin mare for Mr. Dansworth," he said. "Wanna fetch her out for me?"

"The mare isn't for sale," I said. "You know that and so does Dansworth. You'd best get on your horse and get the hell—"

"You got things all wrong," the gunslinger interrupted. "I ain't talkin' about buyin' the mare—I'm talkin' about a little barter between us." He stepped away from his horse, dropping the reins to the ground. The mare stood—she'd been taught to ground-tie.

The gunfighter wore a Colt .45 low an' tied down. He pulled off his gloves by grabbing them with his teeth and let them, too, fall to the ground.

"You got nothin' we want to trade for," I said.

"You can get on your horse an' ride out, or you can ride out dead, tied over your saddle. That ees up to you," Arm said. He took a couple steps away from me, to the side.

The gunslinger went on as if Armando hadn't spoken. "I think we do have somethin' to trade for the horse," he said. "A pair of fat Mex hags an' a surrey. I take the mare with me now an' we let the *putas* go. Simple as that. They'd be back here in an hour, maybe less."

My hand had already dropped to my side, and my fingertips brushed the grips of my Colt. "Where are they?"

The gunfighter was in a pose much like mine, hand hovering near his weapon, his body turned slightly to make a smaller target.

I could barely hear what Arm said. "Lemme have this sumbitch."

I knew Arm's skills. He was pretty fast and his accuracy wasn't bad with his Colt. With his 30.30 he could shoot the tongue out of a sidewinder's mouth at a hundred yards on a moonless night. But against a killer like this one, he didn't have the chance of a snowball in hell. "Not this time, Arm," I said. "I seen this piece of crap cut a man's throat an' gun a sheriff an' deputy in Laredo and I've wanted him for a long time. He's mine, partner."

Arm didn't answer for a moment. Then he said, "Don' make no difference whose bullets kill theese scum, jus' as long as he's dead. Is right, no?"

"Yeah," I said. I met the 'slinger's eyes. "You got a pair of ways to keep on breathing. You mount up an' send our women home, or you tell us where they are an' we go get them. There's nothin' in between."

"Ain't you a cocky pup." The gunfighter grinned. "I guess I gotta tell Mr. Dansworth you fellas wasn't interested in no trade, then. I'll take you both down an' go off with the buckskin. What happens to them Mex women ain't no nevermin' to me."

There's always some sort of a physical rush in a gunfight. The thought of winning and living or losing and dying generates a tingling—a tautness—through a man's body. I saw the gunfighter's fingers grasp the grips of his pistol—but it was like watching one of those stereopticon things, where movement is fast and jerky.

Maybe at one time he'd been very fast. He wasn't any longer—either that, or he was off guard, figuring I was jus' some shit-kicker he'd put a couple slugs into and have plenty of time to drop Arm, as well.

I felt as if a bolt of lightning struck me; everything leaped into a flat-out gallop in my mind and in my body. I could hear my pulse in my ears, feel my heart beat. I saw the gunfighter's Colt begin to leave his holster, until only the barrel was left in the leather. That's as far as it got. I fired three times, putting three bullets into his chest. The impacts threw him back but he didn't go down right away. His fingers released his Colt and it dropped back into his holster. He took half a stumble step back, and then dropped. Three blossoms of red appeared on his shirt and vest. His feet and legs trembled a bit and then were still.

I walked over to his horse, ignoring the corpse, and unbuckled and removed the spade bit from the black mare's mouth. "Let's tie him to his saddle," I said. "His horse'll get him home. He's been around long enough for the mare to know where her stall is. If he comes untied and drops off, the coyotes'll eat good tonight."

"Or *el* buzzards tomorrow. They eat *mierda* such as theese," Arm said.

We didn't want to waste good rope on the killer. We took his gun belt an' Colt but didn't bother going through his pockets or saddlebags. We draped him over his saddle and used baling twine to run a double line under the mare, holding the gunslinger's hands and feet as tight to the horse as possible. The mare was a little jittery; the scent of blood was scaring her. I slapped her on the rump and she skittered away and then began to cut a path toward Hulberton.

"We'd bes' get our horses," Arm said. "We can follow the surrey's tracks good enough—'least to we get to town. Then we see what's what."

I saddled my horse and tugged the Sharps from its scabbard, checking that it was loaded. It was. I replaced the spent cartridges in my Colt and stuck the killer's Colt between my gun belt and my gut. I got a 30.30 from the house an' carried that across my lap once I was mounted.

Arm, too, checked the loads on his Colt and his rifle. We jogged away from the barn. There was really no need to follow the wide-wheeled tracks of the surrey early on; there was only one logical way to make it to the church in town. What we did look for were those tire tracks veering off in any directions, and hoofprints around and near the surrey.

"Tiny, he would like to be here," Arm said.

"He would. But this ain't his fight. The two of us have been able to handle anything thrown at us before. We'll do the same thing this time."

"*Es verdad.*"

It was damned cold and the wind was picking up. There'd been some teasing signs of spring in the last few days, but the temperature and the wind showed us that's all those signs were: teasing. We'd wrapped scarves around our heads to cover our ears and then jammed down our hats to keep the whole mess together. We both wore fingered gloves, but even through them our hands were numbing up some. I was working my fingers almost constantly, clenching and opening my fists to keep the blood running, an' I saw Arm was doing the same thing.

We came upon what we were searching for about forty-five minutes later. At least four men on horseback had come upon the surrey. The tracks there scuffled a good bit; it looked like Teresa and Blanca had tried to make a run for it. They didn't get far. The tracks then showed a man on horseback was leading the surrey horse and that the others were spaced around it.

We rode to the top of a gradual rise and stopped a few hundred yards below what must have been an abandoned farm with a barn that'd caved in on itself. The house was still standing and smoke was leaving the chimney and being immediately

whisked away by the biting wind. Four saddle
horses and the surrey horse were tied to a long
rail in front of the house.

We figured they'd have a couple lookouts and
there were. They were on foot, and their faces
were cherry red from the cold. Neither made an
effort to hide himself. Both cradled rifles.

There was a dim lamp in the farmhouse but
the windows were so dirty we couldn't see any
movement through them. I drew my Sharps and
tied a fresh white pillowcase to it that I'd taken
from the house. "I'll go on down," I said to Arm.
"You watch the lookouts. You see or hear any
shooting, you take them down. Okay?"

"*Sí.*"

I rode to the farmhouse with the barrel of my
Sharps raised, the pillowcase whipping in the
wind.

As I approached, a single man stepped out of
the house, a rifle cradled in his arms, the butt
ready to find his shoulder. I reined to a stop in
front of him.

"Where are the women?" The wind carried
most of my voice away but the fella heard me. I
recognized him from the saloon. He was one of
the cluster that constantly hung about Dansworth.

"They're inside," he said. "Though I gotta say
we ain't any too happy bein' closed in with a
couple of stinkin' Mexicans."

"I want to see them."

"Sure."

He said something over his shoulder and
Blanca and then Teresa were brought past the

now-open door. There was dried blood under Teresa's nose.

"Here's the deal," the kidnapper said. "We go from here to your place with two of my men riding in the surrey with the women. If there's any screwin' around, both *putas* die. Get it? Anything out of the ordinary happens an' they're dead. Then we'll deal with you an' your pard."

He spat a stream of tobacco juice to the ground. "We all go to your place an' git the mare. That's where we let your women go. You try to follow us an' the men already waiting by your place will shoot your asses off."

"How do I know your word is good?"

"You don't—but you got no choice. We're goin' to get that buckskin one way or another. This is the best deal you're gonna git. Take it or leave it."

Before I could answer, he added, "One other thing. I want that Sharps."

"Seems like you got all the cards an' the hand ain't been dealt yet," I said.

"Sure do look like it, don't it." He grinned.

A sudden gust of wind slammed the door inward, giving me a quick view inside. Teresa and Blanca, standing near the fireplace with their arms around each other, were white-faced, either with cold or fear. A fella sat at a rickety table with a bottle in front of him.

I began to speak to the man in front of me—some nonsense about the trade not being fair—and lowered the barrel of my Sharps. I blew a hole through his midsection large enough to ride a draft horse through, let my Sharps fall, and drew my Colt. The man at the table had the bottle to his mouth, upended, sucking whiskey. I was firing rapidly so it was hard to tell which round smashed the bottle, but from the pulp, hair, and crud behind him on the wall, all four of my slugs had taken him in the head.

Teresa and Blanca commenced to scream. Behind me I heard gunfire—two rapid shots, one more—and then silence. Armando's whoop told me he'd taken care of his part of the mission.

The women took some calming down. They'd never seen a gunfight before, much less seen a man catch four rounds from a .45 at close range in his head. Armando rode down and spoke to them in Spanish, touching their shoulders, holding their hands. He was pretty good at it. After maybe fifteen minutes they seemed to have shed all the tears they were going to and some color was returning to their faces. Both refused to cast their eyes anywhere near the wall with the gore still dripping down its rough boards to the floor.

During that fifteen minutes, the wind had begun to pound on the old house, shaking it, bringing forth screams and groans of wood long since overly dry and without real weight-bearing power.

"We gotta git outta here 'fore the whole damn place, she comes down on our heads," Arm warned.

"Yeah. I'll get the surrey an' load up the ladies. You untack the horses this scum rode in on, an' send 'em on their way. Ain't no use in lettin' them freeze to death. 'Least they have a chance to join up with some mustangs."

Neither of us gave a thought to the bodies of

the two lookouts or the pair in the farmhouse—no more than we'd mourn over killing a rat in our barn. In fact, I figured, that's pretty much what we'd done: rid the world of some vermin.

The snow had begun and it was coming on hard, almost parallel to the ground as it was driven by the snarling of the wind. Arm was driving the surrey, jammed between Teresa and Blanca, his horse tied to the back, following the cart. I stayed in my saddle but didn't wander far from the surrey. If we got stuck out here it was the only shelter we had—and piss-poor shelter, at that.

Arm wasn't much good at directions, and neither was I. The best use for a map, we believed, was to tack it up inside an outhouse. We'd operated by instinct and by guessing, but we'd never been in quite a situation as this one. The storm my partner had predicted had fallen on us like a slavering, starving timber wolf.

I could barely see Arm and the women although I was riding a yard away from them. "You know where you're going?" I hollered to Arm.

"Sheet," he yelled back. "I don' know where nada is, Jake."

A brief lapse in the wind allowed me to see Blanca tuck her face very close to Arm's. I could see her mouth moving, but the wind caught up with itself again and I lost any words exchanged.

"Stee close," Armando yelled. "We turn to the left a bit now."

I had no better suggestions so I followed the surrey as it swung in a long arc to the left. It seemed to me that all that accomplished was to give the wind and snow a better bite at my face, but like I said, I had no better suggestions.

I lost all sense or orientation or direction; I might just as well have been ridin' on the surface of the damned moon. I'd gone a couple feet beyond the surrey horse, because I had no idea what sort of obstacle he could get tangled in—rock outcroppings, snowdrifts, whatever-the-hell, and I was in a much better position to handle my animal than Arm was with the surrey horse and the long reins.

I began to think of making a shelter from the surrey; tip it on its side, break off a few boards, and tie the horses in snug enough so that they'd make a sort of a wall. I couldn't see a damned thing, and I was just about to turn to yell to Arm about building, pulling in, and waiting out the worst of the storm, when my horse walked into the side of our barn.

Chapter Seven

I figured it had to be our barn; there were no other barns around our land that were still standing, and even if it wasn't ours, it'd provide better shelter from the lashing wind and whiteout snow.

The thing is, although I knew it was a barn, I had no idea where we positioned on it. A couple feet from the main door? The very back of the structure? One of the sides?

There was only one way to find out: dismount, tie my horse to the surrey, and start walking, keeping at least one hand on the wood siding. That wasn't nearly as easy as it sounded—the wind was doing its level best to tear my legs out from under me. I imagined myself being whisked away like a tumbleweed, to die in a snowbank.

I climbed down from my horse and followed the traces of the surrey to Arm and handed my reins to him. I leaned in close. "I'm gonna follow the siding until I come to a door an' then I'll be back to get you. Ain't no other way to do it." Arm shouted something but the storm carried his words away before they reached me.

I took short steps, facing the barn, both hands in contact with it. It was hard and clumsy walking. I fell a couple of times, tripping over things

I couldn't see. There was a flash of panic each time: suppose I rolled or was blown away from the structure. I had no choice. I went on.

Actually, we were fairly fortunate. We'd struck the barn on the north side, not many feet from where the rectangle made its turn to the front. The feel of that big sliding door was wonderful. I backtracked just as slowly as I'd come to the door and walked into the side of my horse. I grabbed the surrey horse's bit with one hand and set out again, retracing my path to the door, one hand always in contact with the wood.

The door was a bitch to open with the wind blowing against it, but I got it open wide enough for the surrey to pass through. The wood inside screamed under the stress of the storm, and it was as cold as a tomb, but we were out of the wind. I muscled the door closed while Arm fumbled around near the tack room, scouting for one of the lamps we kept hanging here and there. He found one, lit it, and the light shoved the darkness aside.

Blanca and Teresa were making the sign of the cross and praying, seemingly frozen to their seat.

"I gotta bring the mustang in," I told Arm. "There's no way we can build anything to keep him outta the wind."

My partner's lips were blue and numb. He mumbled rather than spoke. "Always with hand on wood," he managed to get out. I nodded. "You need rope for open space."

He was right. The corral wasn't tight to the barn—there was fifty feet or so between them. I took a double wrap of rope around my waist and tied it off and then tied the other end around a stout upright beam. I went out again. The damned storm hadn't abated a hair. I stumbled and cursed my way in what I thought was a fairly straight line until I hit the corral. I was fairly close to the singing gate.

I didn't have to find the stallion—he found me, shoving his muzzle against my chest. I guess it was as if we'd declared a temporary truce; we weren't going to argue when our lives were at stake. I grabbed his halter with one hand and drew on the rope, reeling us in like a pair of big fish being hauled out of a river. I led him through the barn door and pulled him into a box stall. He stood there shaking, eyes huge, looking around, a long icicle suspended from his lower lip, his muzzle frosted, eyelashes thick with snow. I secured the gate and tossed him some hay.

Arm had put both our horses and the surrey horse into stalls and had hayed them. Our work wasn't yet over and we both knew that. We had to run a line between the barn and the house. That didn't take too long; we were oriented and it would have been hard to miss the house. We knotted the rope around the hitching post by the porch and followed it back to the barn. Teresa and Blanca were still praying, huddled together, the chatter of their teeth making their Spanish sound like some strange language from Europe or somewheres.

We led the ladies to the house. The first thing they did—even before taking off their heavy coats—was to add wood to the stove fire with trembling hands. The first thing Arm did—before taking off his coat—was to fumble a bottle of whiskey out of the cabinet with his trembling hands, yanked the cork with his teeth, and took a very long drink. Then, he handed the bottle to me. I did the same.

Outside, the storm continued with demonic malevolence. We heard sounds of pain and protest from our farmhouse we'd never heard before, and the power of the wind was such that the entire house shivered, trembled, like the ground does when a highballin' train roars by a few feet away from a man. Still, it was cozy enough inside. We built a huge fire in the fireplace while the women—still uttering prayers—heated up some stew and put biscuits up to rise. Arm and I had another belt or maybe two and then went to our rooms and changed out of our frozen clothing.

When we came down, something was tickling Armando's mind. "Tell me theese," he said to Blanca. "How you know to make that beeg swing that got us home. Nobody could see nada, yet you . . ."

"You are too far away from your people," Blanca said, "to remember what a *niño's* job was, no? My family, we made pulque—thee good pulque, not thee rotgut. The only agave we used was thee leetle short ones that grew in the shadow of the arms of the beeg cactus—the primo agave. The *niños*, we would be sent out in the morning with a burlap sack as big as we were an' we no come back 'til the sack, it is full. We took a mule, no? An' we went miles an' miles searching out the right plants. If we no make sure where we were alla time—well, it wasn't good. Some died.

It became natural we do this—an' many of us, we still can do it."

"Some of the times we'd cut the head from a rattlesnake and toss heem inna sack," Teresa added. "It makes good flavor in the pulque."

That pulque is a kinda frothy stuff that tastes like scorpion piss, an' it'll knock a big man down faster than a .45 will. I never had much use for it; I drank it once an' woke up a day later with my boots, money, pistol, an' horse gone.

"One must know how to drink cactus juice, Jake," Arm said.

"Yer ass. Ain't nobody who can drink that stuff an' remain standing."

"Beely, he drink it."

"Sure, Billy the Kid drank it an' he shot three men in a saloon for no goddamn reason. Don't tell me about no pulque, Arm. It's poison."

There's only so much that can be done around a farm—particularly one with only a few animals—during the cruelest and coldest part of a West Texas winter. I was handling, fondling, and grooming our stallion daily. The stud was coming along nicely. He'd get a little nervous and antsy when I kept him in a stall for too long a time, I guess because in the course of his life he'd never been boxed in, and although he enjoyed the grub and the attention, he preferred to be outside in his shelter in the corral. The mare was an easy keeper; she required little attention but obviously appreciated the daily grooming. The foal was curious and affable and I'd often let him out in the aisle in the middle of the barn to wander and sniff and see what the world was 'bout. He followed me like a puppy tagging along after his master.

Arm bought a load of lumber and replaced any cracked or warped boards. Beyond that he pestered Blanca and Teresa, following them as they went about their chores. When he attempted to advise them on their cooking, they'd had more than enough of him and laid into him in shrill and vindictive Spanish. I couldn't understand any of it, but poor Armando slunk out of the kitchen with his tail 'tween his legs.

If those two ladies were men, I don't doubt that Arm would have hurt them badly—or worse.

We rode into town one fine day, when the sky was as blue as it ever got and there wasn't a cloud in sight. Even the wind had died and the sun was shining with July intensity, although with none of its heat. Our horses were frisky, nodding their heads to get under their bits and run off some steam. We wanted to let them run—we knew how they felt—but it was too dangerous. The snow that appeared as flat and level as an ironing board could hide rocks, holes, and ruts that could bust a leg.

Tiny, as usual, was happy to see us. We visited his shop, put up our horses there, and watched as he finished nailing new shoes on a typey-looking carriage gelding. Then, 'course, we meandered over to the saloon.

We hadn't seen Dansworth since we freed Blanca and Teresa. I'd kind of expected immediate retaliation, but nothing happened for a few weeks and Arm and I had pretty much put the whole episode out of mind, just as if we'd done nothing more than plugged a few rats around our grain barrels.

The tender brought us our usual tray: a bottle of decent whiskey and six foaming schooners of cold beer. We settled in at a rickety table. Tiny told us a long tale of how he'd once ridden a Tennessee walking horse, and how that animal's gait was as smooth as rolling slowly in a sweet, sweet, lady's arms.

As usual, Dansworth and a cluster of his boys were at the rear of the saloon. They seemed drunker than they generally were, but we paid little attention to them. Arm was in the middle of a story of how his pa's mule once sat down midday and refused to work. Mules or horses don't sit like dogs or cats do, 'course, an' what Arm's pa done was to take a wooden match, slide it into that ornery mule's bung, an' touched it off with another. That mule never gave his pa another minute of trouble, but from then on, he carried his tail like one of them Arabian horses—up an' arced. We were having a laugh when Dansworth strode over to our table and stood there, glaring down at me.

I'd drawn my .45 under the table when I saw him begin our way and I was pretty certain Arm had, too.

Dansworth's stance was good and steady, but his eyes showed he was drunk. I looked him up an' down. He had a day or so of stubble on his face, his shirt and coat were wrinkled, and his drawers had some stains. What I focused on, though, was his .45 and his gun belt. I know prime leatherwork when I see it, an' Dansworth's was the best. The stitches were so tight together on his holster it was hard to see they were anything other'n a single line. I know the difference between bone an' ivory, and his weapon's grips were ivory. His hand was loose next to the pistol, fingers curved in a tad.

The entire saloon went as quiet as the inside of a long-in-the-ground coffin.

"You cost me some more good men," he said. His words weren't slurred at all, but damn, his eyes were drunk.

"Good men?" I said mildly. "I cost you nothing. See, I don't consider anyone who grabs up women an' holds 'em up for ransom to be men. All I did was drop some trash onto the ground."

The silence in the joint continued. Dansworth continued his stare at me.

"I'm faster an' better than you've ever been," he said. "I had me a—"

"You had a fine pistol built from the ground up," I said. "And the cut of your holster makes it easy to get to that fine .45. I hear a gunman taught you to handle a gun. That's fine. But, you piece of horseshit, on the best day you ever had, in a gunfight 'tween you an' me, you'd go down an' die. That's the way things are, Dansworth."

The drunkenness from his eyes finally reached his mouth. "Y . . . You think you can . . ."

I let the hammer forward on my Colt. There wasn't going to be a gunfight here. I didn't holster my pistol, but it'd take more than a puffball to hit the trigger to fire it.

"You come back sober an' maybe we'll talk about this—maybe do something about it."

"You think I . . . I can't . . ."

"I know you can't. Right now you couldn't shoot Jumbo the goddamn elephant if he pinched your nose."

Dansworth turned and walked back to his crew. They huddled together for a few minutes and then one, a hatchet-faced fella with a patch over one eye, came to our table. "Mr. Dansworth, he says you're chickenshit, Walters. He says he'll bet you a thousand dollars cash he can outshoot you right here an' right now."

I was getting tired of this folderol. "I don't care to draw on drunks. Tell Walters that if—"

"No, that ain't the bet," the one-eyed man said. "We'll set up six shot glasses on that beam back by our table. You an' Mr. Dansworth stand back about thirty feet an' do your shootin'. Whoever busts the most shot glasses wins."

I was about to tell him to go to hell when I glanced over at Arm. He was grinnin' like a Halloween punkin. So was Tiny.

"Our table here," I said, "is maybe fifty feet from that beam. Dansworth shoots from thirty feet an' I'll shoot from here. This is for a thousand, cash, right? Fair 'nuff?"

One-eye near busted a gut scurryin' back to the rear of the saloon with my offer.

Dansworth's "Goddamn fool," and his laugh were louder than the rabble around him. He dispatched a man to the bar to fetch a dozen shot glasses an' to set six up a few inches apart on the beam. Then Dansworth, grinning, took thirty paces toward us.

"Them las' steps, they was kinda short," Arm pointed out.

"Let it go," I said.

Dansworth turned his back on us. Again, the gin mill was totally silent. He shrugged his shoulders, clenched and unclenched his right fist, spat off to one side, an' drew his .45. The explosions of his rounds were like dynamite in the closed building. Dansworth fired quickly—maybe a bit too quickly. Five of the shot glasses shattered but one remained standing, as if mocking him. Still he seemed satisfied with his performance and his boys whistled, whooped, and cheered.

I hadn't taken into consideration the murkiness of the air in the saloon, which had been increased by the smoke from Dansworth's pistol. I could barely see the new shot glasses that'd been set up. The outlaws backed away—far away—from the beam and my diminutive targets. I pretended to check the load in my .45 as I scrambled for a plan. The only one I could up with was not only risky but foolish, but it's all I had. After all, if I couldn't see my targets, I couldn't very well hit them. I stood and pushed my chair back, .45 hanging easily, comfortably in my hand. I looked things over once again and fired my first round. The kerosene lamp hanging a few feet from where Dansworth stood detonated nicely, casting more than enough orangish white light for my purposes. I picked off the next four glasses with no trouble at all. Then came the challenge. I fired my sixth shot so that it hit and smashed the very edge of the sixth glass, but blew enough glass at the fifth to bust it up. I let out a breath I'd been holding.

"Holy sheet!" Armando exclaimed.

"Some shootin', Jake," Tiny added. "I never seen nothin' like it."

If the truth be known, I probably couldn't pull off that little trick again in a thousand tries, but that didn't matter none. It worked this time.

I remained standing and Arm stood, too, and moved several feet to my left. The buzz and snarls from the other end of the saloon were as ominous as the warning of a rattlesnake. I knew this thing wasn't over, an' so did Arm.

After a few moments the one-eyed, hatchet-faced fella walked toward us, headed to Arm rather than to me. I looked him over. His .45 was tied low on his leg and his holster was well-worn. He had a sheath of banknotes in his left hand. He stopped about eight feet from Arm. "This here's your pard's money, Pancho," he said. He opened his hand and the bills fluttered to the floor. "All you gotta do is pick 'em up with your teeth and you'll walk out of here. You don't, you'll be carried out—dead." He paused for a moment and smiled. "Pretend they're tamales, Pancho—that'll make it somethin' you're used to doin'."

Armando grinned. "S'pose I put a slug right on through that patch over your eye," he said, his voice conversational, calm. "An' then I pick up the money?"

"Well, lemme tell you somethin', Pancho. See, what I'm offerin' . . ."

It was a gunfighter's trick that was already old

when Methuselah was a infant. Get the opponent to shift his mind for the tiniest part of a second and draw then. His hand flashed to the grips of his Colt.

There was one round fired. Arm's slug passed on through the black cloth patch. A spurt of blood and grayish glop spat out of hatchet-face's eye socket and a sizable piece of the back of his head sailed the length of the room, struck the wall, and stuck there to the rough wood. I drew and kept my pistol leveled on Dansworth's group. Arm picked up the cash. I nodded to Tiny and the three of us backed on out.

For once, Dansworth had no parting words.

Tiny was pale-faced as we stood out in the street, the wind snapping grit and discarded newspaper pages past us. "Maybe I oughta start carryin' iron," he said.

Arm's voice was low and serious. "Don't even theenk of it, amigo. Jake an' me, we been doin' this all our lives, no? You know the Bible? It says, 'He who lives by the sword, dies by the sword.' Ees good advice."

"You start carryin'," I said, "an' you'd kill two men."

"Two? I . . ."

"*Sí. Es verdad.* You an' the man who killed you. Me an' Jake, we take him down."

Tiny looked up at the sky. "You boys got some daylight left. Let's put a dent in my tequila supply an' talk this over."

The low fire in the forge provided all the heat we needed. Arm an' me sat on bales of hay, but

Tiny was antsy, pacing. We passed his bottle of tequila around a couple of times.

"I take me a deer whenever I need meat," Tiny said. "A bear killed two of my best dogs an' I put a dozen shots into the sumbitch, but I killed him. I ain't new to guns, boys."

"You're new to handguns, Tiny," I said. "And you're brand-new to takin' the life of another man if it ever come to that. 'Course you kill a deer for meat, an' that bear, an' a barrel fulla rattlesnakes an' rats to boot."

"*Sí*," Arm said. "Keeling a man is different. I dream sometimes about gunfights an' I sweat an' sometimes I cry."

"Yeah, Tiny," I said. "It ain't just a matter of bein' a little faster an' pullin' a trigger. The boys who died had mas and pas an' maybe wives an' children. Sometimes . . . sometimes . . . I wish I'd lost."

Tiny sucked the bottle for a long moment. "Jake—if you'd lost, then Arm woulda settled the score. Isn't that right?"

"Score? Bullshit. There ain't no score in gunfighting. We do what we gotta do."

"So—if a 'slinger dropped you, he'd jus' ride away?"

"No," Arm said. Tiny and I waited a moment but Arm didn't say anything else and it was clear he wasn't going to.

"We gotta saddle up," I said eventually. "And for a while, we gotta cut out our trips to town— the two of us together, I mean. Dansworth knows we'd track him down if he grabbed our mare, but we can't leave the place unprotected." I turned to Tiny. "You're our very good friend," I said. "You'll have to come to us 'stead of us comin' to you—but you do that whenever you take a mind to. Hear? Anytime at all. We have whiskey an' food an' we want you to be free to come by anytime."

The air took on a fresh sweetness not long thereafter, and the melting snow runoff sounded like a distant river. Gutsy grass sprigs began to poke their heads through the remaining snow and here and there were good-size patches of rich-looking mud and soil. Riding in the mud loosened shoes quickly, kinda of sucked them away from the hoof with each stride. Both of us could renail a shoe, so it was no trouble. The smith skills—shaping a show from bar stock, leveling it, screwing on nubs for traction, all that, was beyond us. A lame horse is as useless as teats on a boot heel; we took our horses to Tiny for that kind of work.

Our stallion was gettin' as nervous as a whore in church, sniffing the spring air, hustling about in his corral as if he expected a magic door to suddenly appear, giving him freedom.

I worked him daily on a long rope, running around me at the end of the rope at a pretty good clip, even with that stumble-footed gait of his. He hadn't offered to attack me in quite some time, but I was still leery. He'd been born in the wild and had gone where he wanted to when he wanted to his entire life. I doubt that he'd ever get used to captivity. He was looking good. He'd filled out some and his coat had taken on an almost brassy shine to it. The work on the rope kept him muscled up and tight.

The mare was looking good, too. She was showing that she was pregnant and that the youngster had moved back inside her toward her birth canal. She ate almost nonstop, but we figured she was eating for two, and let her have at good hay and grain. It put some fat on her but we'd work that off after she'd given birth.

Neither Arm nor me had much experience with birthing. We'd see it happen now and again on our travels, but knew little about the process.

Arm rode into Hulberton to borrow a couple books on the process from Tiny and to discuss the whole procedure with him. Arm did better than that—he and Tiny rode in late that night, drunk, laughing, having a hell of a time, with a sack of thick books in Arm's saddlebags. The ladies hustled about in the kitchen preparing a fine meal of venison stew and mashed potatoes, biscuits to sop with, canned tomatoes, and all sorts of treats, an' then left us alone. We ate like three sows at a trough and our bottle took some hard use, too.

Dansworth, Tiny told us, had bought a string of eight horses from a couple of Mexican traders. There were a couple of nice mares and one stud that looked good—but not near as good as our stud. He—Dansworth—was still running his mouth about owning our mare. Tiny said it looked like he'd added a few more saddlebums and drifters to his army.

The next morning Tiny looked over the mare very carefully. He said it was time to start keeping her tail wrapped and to grease up her exterior womb a bit with udder balm daily. He felt of her gut an' said the foal was a big 'un, but she looked like she could pass it okay when the time came. We studied the books at the kitchen table an' Tiny told us what supplies to have on hand an' how to cut the cord right and clean the afterbirth and all that. He told us how the mare would act when she was about due, and how her teats would wax up, a sure sign birth wasn't far off. We kept a pair of large buckets of water simmering on the stove at all times, and a tall stack of freshly laundered towels outside the stall. One of the buckets was for us to wash our hands with if we had to reach inside her to help things along, and there was a big chunk of lye soap on a shelf above the bucket.

Tiny asked that one of us come to town and fetch him when the mare started contractions and we promised we would—very gratefully.

Teresa an' Blanca were excited about the bambino and spent lots of time talking to and stroking the *mamacita*. The mare just ate up the extra attention, grunting and sighing and poking about for the treats the ladies brought in their aprons—like carrots and quartered apples.

It hadn't rained much this spring and the ground was fairly well dried out. I was standing in the stud's corral near the snubbing post, moving dirt around with the toe of my boot. The horse was antsy, looking for action, bored with his life, I suppose. I thought I'd given him some new sort of exercise. I hooked the rope to his halter and led him up tight to the post. Then, I went into the barn.

Arm was rewrapping the mare's tail as I hefted my stock saddle an' blanket an' started back out to the corral.

"You are nots, no?" he said. "You canno ride that horse, Jake. *Jesús*."

"I'm not 'nots'—I just wanna give him a little exercise, is all. I know he'll never be a ridin' horse 'cause of that hoof—but, well—what the hell. Won't hurt to set on him for a second."

"An' get your seely neck busted."

I ignored that.

I'd been sacking out the stallion for several weeks, so the feel of the blanket on his back was no big deal. He eyed my saddle, however, like it were about to attack an' eat him. Arm had followed me out and was untying the bandana from around his neck. He sidled up to the horse, stood there for a moment, and then, quickly and smoothly had the bandana over the stud's eyes and tied under his jaw. I'd tied a short length of rope to the halter to use as a rein.

I eased the saddle onto the horse's back as if I were settling it on a giant, fragile egg. The stud went stiff and began to tremble as I pulled the cinch. I put my hand in a stirrup and pressed down some. The stud's trembling increased—it was as if his whole body was in motion.

"He gonna come apart," Arm said quietly.

My partner was right. A few more seconds and his fear of the weight on him would overcome his fear of blindness and he'd explode. I put a boot into a stirrup and swung into the saddle, calling, "Pull!" to Arm. He unsnapped the rope from the halter and yanked the bandana free.

We stood statue-still for the barest part of a second and then the horse went up like one of those Chinese Fourth of July rockets. He came down hard, but I could feel that he kept weight off the twisted hoof. He went up again, higher yet, and came down with his weight on his rear hooves, as if he was rearing. I kicked out of the stirrups so's I could push free if I had to. I'd rather hit the dirt like a sack of grain than do the same thing with 1,200 pounds of horse on top of me.

It seemed like we stood there forever, my hands and arms stiff against the saddle horn to push off if I needed to, my legs free. Then we were in motion again, leaping forward. I was shifting all over the saddle until I was able to get my boots back into the stirrups.

I'd expected a spin, and I got it. The stallion spun away from his lame foot, and the sumbitch went around as fast as one of them tops kids play with. He stopped faster than a horse in a spin can stop, and my momentum carried my upper body forward—particularly my head. My nose slammed into the horse's poll—the space between his ears—and I was immediately choking on blood. The only thing louder than the stud's bellows-like wheezing and gasping for air was Arm's laughter.

I'd like to say I rode that hellhound to a standstill. I didn't. He spun again and went up again and that was pretty much it for me. I was seeing little black spots in front of my eyes from the blow to my face and I was dizzy and off balance. I hit the ground like a cow flop and Arm hustled over to me in case the horse wanted to play some

more. He didn't—he rolled on the ground until
he busted my cinch and ran to the far wall of the
corral, head hanging, sweat dripping, sides
heaving.

"You give him a good ride, amigo," Arm said.

I couldn't think of an answer.

I ended up with a nose that was at least twice
its normal size that hurt like a sonofabitch, and a
pair of black eyes that made me look like a rac-
coon. Other than that, I came through my ride
pretty well. Tequila and a long night's sleep didn't
hurt, either. A taste of tequila the following morning helped out. Teresa made a poultice for my
nose that tied around my face like a mask. I have
no idea what she put in it, but it sure cut the pain
way down.

Right about this time the mare began to bag up,
which makes her udder begin to swell. We
weren't sure if all was right, so Arm rode into
town and brought Tiny back with him. He looked
her over, checked her tail wrapping, and nodded
with satisfaction when he saw how clean the
stray in the birthing stall was, and that we'd
nailed lamps at each corner of the stall, high
enough to be well out of the way, but in good position to cast all the light we should need.

Tiny washed his hands real good in the hot
water, lathering up with the lye soap. He gently
touched her teats and grinned when she didn't
react. "Some of 'em get right tetchy about now,
but this gal don't pay no mind. That's good. You
boys wash her teats a couple times a day with
warm water from now on, hear?"

Tiny felt of her rear stomach and between her

legs. "She ain't gonna have no trouble or I miss my bet," he said. "Everything is where it's supposed to be. Sometimes you get a breech birth—the ass end of the foal comes out first—but that ain't gonna happen here."

"She is okay, no?" Arm asked.

"She's good. Real good. Next thing'll happen is her udder'll start to fill out. You already seen a little wax on her nipples; that'll get a lot thicker as her time comes. Lotsa thick wax usually means you'll have a foal in a day or so, give or take. She'll probably get a little nervous, maybe kinda pace in her stall. That's okay. If she stops chowing down like regular, that's a good sign, too."

Tiny came out of the stall and faced Arm and me. "Lookit here. Mares have foaled for lots of years without you two screwin' around tryin' to help. She's gonna do fine. Let her be." We nodded.

Tiny had several horses to shoe and a couple of oxen needed resets so he went on back to town. Arm an' me stood around the birthing stall not saying much. We were a whole lot more nervous than that good mare.

The whole thing went perfectly, naturally, just as Tiny said it would. The mare went down on her side after her water busted and she moaned some and squealed a couple of times as the pains hit her. We could see her muscles flex as she pushed.

A front foot came out of her canal and then a half minute later the other one followed, maybe four or five inches behind the first. When the forelegs were out to the knees, we saw the nose—and then the snout—and then the entire head.

It was the most beautiful thing me or Arm had ever seen.

When she'd passed the shoulders out she rested, sucking air, moaning every now and again. I wanted to jump into the stall and hold her head in my lap and tell her what a great and brave girl she was, but I stayed where I belonged, outside the stall.

Their was a gauzy, wet, slick white sack all around the foal that the mother kinda nipped to break open. She rested again, breathing hard, and then passed the hindquarters and rear legs. The cord was still attached and we left it alone, just as Tiny told us to. He said at that point, it was passing blood and stuff between mother and foal. After a bit of licking and cleaning of her baby, the mare struggled to her feet and the cord broke like a piece of light, wet rope snapping. Later, I said it made a little noise but Arm said it didn't, and his hearing was better than mine.

It wasn't but fifteen or so minutes later that the foal lurched to his feet and nuzzled about for a teat to suck. He was shaky on his feet and his legs were just plain silly-looking things—like thin tan sticks that could never hold the weight of his body, but did. While the baby sucked, his ma pushed out a mass of placenta.

And that was it. The Busted Thumb Horse Ranch had its first foal—a colt with a light bay color to him. Armando and I shook hands. We both had tears in our eyes and on our faces and neither of us were the least embarrassed.

You'd think neither of us had seen a mare or a foal before, we spent so much time gawking into the birthing stall. We cleaned out the straw with the stuff on it—blood, yellowish liquid, and particularly the afterbirth, which smelled like very sour milk. The mare was protective but not aggressive. I knew a fella in Burnt Rock who'd had his sweetest mare shatter his knee when he was toweling down a foal, and me an' Arm realized that the maternal instinct was strong. We were real careful around the foal and his ma—but we never had a minute of trouble.

Spring came on nicely an' our mare was getting hungry for that that fresh grass she could smell coming up outside. Also, the lady was bored, and I couldn't blame her. Standing in a stall with a kid doin' his best to suck you dry couldn't have been a real good time. The foal was bored, too; he started nipping at his ma, waiting 'til she was asleep an' then pestering her, and so forth.

Arm and I built an acre or so of fence while the digging was easy, while the ground was still pretty wet. We set 4'×4' posts two feet deep and ran good, stout, parallel boards—three of them, one close to the ground so the foal couldn't slide out an' go exploring.

We turned the pair of them out on a spring day that was like a day in heaven—lotsa sun, a perfectly blue sky, an' not a breeze even whispering. The mare hauled ass around that little corral, kicking, squealing, running hard, havin' a grand time. The foal tried to keep up with her but he didn't have a chance.

Finally, when his ma was finished celebrating and was tearing up that fresh grass, the foal caught her and began to suck. He looked at that sweet green grass a few times, nuzzled it once, and then went back to the teat.

I'll tell you, it was a pure pleasure to watch.

The ladies needed supplies and I hooked up their rig for them. We argued a tad about the amount of liquor I ordered, but they finally gave in. It'd been a while since they'd been to Hulberton 'cause the big wheels on their rig were bound to find places to sink into up to their hubs or more. Arm gave them a bunch of money—I don't know how much—an' sent them on their way.

They seemed awful happy to get away from their daily chores, me, Arm, and the whole ranch.

Arm had gone out on his horse to ride the land a bit. When he came back, he told me he'd found a lot of tracks indicating we'd been watched for a good time. That was no surprise. Both of us had seen a pair or so of Dansworth's flunkies riding our borders throughout the hard weather.

As spring came, the riders came closer. They seemed to spend a good amount of time on a rocky rise that'd give them a good view of both the mare and the foal, and the stud in his corral.

Arm and I were in the barn an' he was unsaddling his horse. "We need some help," he said. "They weel come, no? You've insulted Dansworth, we've keeled his men, he wants our horse."

"We've got rifles at every goddamn window in the house an' in the barn. We've got more ammo than—"

"*Dos* men fight a army? Ees stupid, my brother. You know that."

"We never needed no help before, Arm. We can—"

"Estupido. We both die, our horses are gone, our ranch is burned. No?"

"No."

The argument was ended abruptly by the sound of Blanca and Teresa screaming and the clatter and bang of a rig being pushed too hard over bad ground. They dragged to a stop in front of the barn, the horses sweating and heaving, both women yelling at once.

"Tiny—he is shoot! They shoot Tiny!"

"I'll go into town, Arm—you gotta stay here to keep watch. My horse is fresh."

"We ride together," he growled.

"No, dammit, not this time we don't. I'm going to check on Tiny an' then find out where the nearest telegraph office is. I guess maybe you're right. We need help. I'm gonna call in some debts."

"Who you wire?"

"I'm not sure—I gotta think on that."

"Tiny is how bad?" Arm asked the women.

"He has bullets in him an' is no talking but was breath—breathing. We don' know no more."

I was saddling my horse. "You ladies stay inside no matter what. Arm—I don't know what's going to happen but it ain't gonna be good. Keep a close watch but stick to the barn, okay?"

"Sí. Any Dansworth men come here, they die."

I urged my horse harder than I should have, taking crazy shortcuts over snow that could have hidden rocks and holes that would have broken both our necks if we hit on wrong.

I had to slow a few times to let my horse blow and suck fresh air, but like I've said before, he was a hell of a ride an' he gave me the best he had that day. We pulled up in front of Tiny's shop and I turned my horse into the corral an' dashed inside. The fire in Tiny's forge was completely out, which wasn't a good sign. A few men I didn't recognize stood around Tiny's cot. I pushed through them and jolted to a stop. Tiny's body was covered completely with a sheet.

"When? Who?" I asked, my voice cracking with both wrath and sorrow.

One of the men, his face tear-stained, answered. "Late last night. I heard the shots an' come runnin' over. Tiny, I think he was already gone. He was fulla lead—they musta emptied their guns into him—the dirty sonsabitches."

I stepped ahead and gently lifted the cloth from my friend's face and brought it down to his waist. He was still dressed. He'd taken several shots to the head and his shirt had a good dozen bloody holes in it. I put the sheet back.

"You boys get the undertaker here an' get Tiny in a box. I'll pay for everything—make sure he's cleaned up so he can be buried decent. If he doesn't have a casket big enough, have him make one—a damn good one." I handed over whatever money I had in my pocket. "This'll get things started. Now—where's the nearest telegraph office?"

An ol' fella—one I'd seen around the shop an' the saloon—said, "Couple hours east in Big Bell. There's a railroad depot there, too."

I picked a tall gray from a stall who was muscled up good an' looked like he could cover ground. Rasp marks on his hooves showed he'd just been shod. I grabbed a stock saddle off a rack and fit it on him. I put a low-level port in his mouth an' led him outta his stall.

"One of you fellas untack my horse an' rub him down good. Feed an' grain him, but not too much water at first. I'll pay . . ."

"You won't pay nothin'," the ol' man said. "Tiny was a good man—the best. Hell, it's a honor to see to your horse, Mr. Jake. You go on to Big Bell an' do what you gotta do."

I guess it was pretty clear what I needed a telegraph office for. One of the men said, " 'Member—Dansworth's boys are hard cases an' killers. You get the best men you can, boys who ain't afraid of tradin' lead."

I nodded. "You can bet on that." I mounted up and set off east, getting the feel of the gray. He had even, strong gaits and the rocking-chair lope of a good quarter horse. His gallop was damned near as fast as that of my own horse. He broke a sweat right away, but his breathing stayed even an' he took whatever gait I asked for without a touch of trouble.

I'd picked a hell of a good ride. This boy would get me to Big Bell as fast as any horse I ever rode, 'cept my own. I held him to a lope, figurin' who might be where, and whether I'd be able to reach as many men as I wanted to. Lots of our friends had paper on them, a few must have been killed or jailed since we last saw them, and others were drifters who kept moving, not headed anywhere in particular. Still, I was sure my offer of real good money an' the fact that many—or most—of these fellas had some kind of debt—not money, but the important kind of debt, like jail bustin' an' gunfightin'—to me an' Arm.

There were somewhere between a dozen an' twenty of these boys I figured I could reach out to. All of them were gunmen, killers—an' all of them paid their debts. Some were a touch crazy, either from the war or 'cause they were born that way, but that made no nevermind. I could trust these fellas an' I knew not a one of them would hesitate to pull a trigger on an enemy of Armando or me.

I ran into a light, misty rain that made footing a bit more precarious, but didn't slow our pace. We made it to Big Bell. I dropped the gray at the stable to be walked and rubbed down, found out where the telegraph office was, and ran to it, my boots squishing an' sliding in the mud.

Chapter Eight

It seems to me that every telegraph operator I've ever seen looked like a damn mouse, and this fella was no exception. He had vaguely brown hair, which was thinning, and a sharp face with an even sharper nose. His shoulders slumped forward like those of a mouse, too, probably from leaning over his key all day. He was probably as strong as a fried egg.

He looked up at me briefly when I walked in and then went back to his tip-tapping. I was dressed like a cowhand and he apparently had more important things to do than fiddle about with a saddlebum.

I'd figured out who I wanted to contact and sat at a little table and wrote each name and the best address I could come up with on a little yellow sheet of paper provided for customers, using the pencil on the table. My message was the same to each man:

Me and Arm in trouble. Need help right now. Will pay big. Bring ammo. Jake Walters's horse farm. Hulberton, W. Texas. Ask in town.

I read over my work and thought it wasn't half

bad. It said what I wanted it to say without a bunch of useless greetings an' such folderol.

I walked over to where the operator sat behind the same kind of window a bank teller uses.

"I need this to go out right away—now."

The mouse looked up at me with oily little dark eyes. "This is my busiest time of the day," he said, as if he were talking to a worm. "Stop back in the morning if . . ."

I drew my pistol, spun it in my hand, and smashed the mouse's window with the butt. Then I grabbed his tie an' lifted him out of his chair. "I said now and I meant now. That other horseshit can wait."

"B . . . but I can't possibly . . ."

"Here's what we'll do," I said. "You'll either send my messages now or I'll shove your little key thing up your scrawny ass." I let go of his tie and he fell back into his chair. I reached into my back pocket and put some twenties on his table. "That oughta cover it. Start sendin'."

It took the rodent better'n two hours to get all sixteen messages sent. As he worked, fat drops of sweat rolled down his forehead, although it was cool in the little office.

"There," he said. He started adding figures on a sheet of paper next to him. "Like I said, all them twenties will cover it. You keep the change."

I fetched Tiny's horse from the stable, paid up, and rode back to Hulberton. I didn't push the gray on the way back, but he held that lope beautifully. I couldn't help thinking it was too bad he was a gelding. If he had his eggs, covering our mare with him might give us another fine foal. That got me thinking about Tiny . . .

He slugged down half a schooner of beer, his grin as wide as Texas. "So the doc hands the fella a big bottle fulla thick brown liquid that smelled an' tasted like goat dung. 'This here'll take care of ya,' the doc says. 'Slug the whole bottle on down.'

"Now the poor cowhand figured this doc knew what he was doin', so he set to drinkin' from the bottle, damn near pukin' as he did. Well, finally, he got 'er all down.

"'There,' the doc says, 'that'll take care of your cramps.'

"'Cramps!' the cowhand yells, 'I said crabs!'"

I laughed, blowing beer outta my nose. Arm sat there looking from Tiny to me, stone-faced. "Crabs? What is this crabs?"

"Bush bunnies," Tiny laughed.

"Boosh bonnies?"

"Bugs, Arm," I said. "Ball bugs."

"Ahhh. Then why didn't the cowhand say that? Why he say . . ."

"Let it go, Arm," I suggested.

"Ees boolshit," he said. "Domb Anglo joke."

I shook my head, which made my horse a touch nervous, but he calmed down and so did I. I reined him in just a hair and I saw the tracks we'd left going the other way. It made me shudder. Anyone riding like that through the snow-covered, treacherous terrain we covered hadda be a idjit.

We made it because we had to.

I was maybe a hair nervous as I approached the farm. Arm had all the lamps in the barn on. Most of the lanterns in the house were on 'cept in Teresa an' Blanca's room. They were dark.

A slug hissed over my head a half second before I heard the shot fired.

"Goddammit," I yelled out, "Arm, it's me!"

"I thought so—is why I shoot high."

I rode up to the barn and dismounted. Arm had a 30.30 over his shoulder an' a half-empty bottle of tequila in his left hand. There's no easy way to say what I had to say. "Tiny's dead. He had a lot of lead in him."

Arm held my gaze for a long moment. "Tiny, he never carried no gun. We jus' talked about that. 'Member?"

My partner turned away from me for a moment and swiped his sleeve across his eyes. He turned back and said, "We will no let theese go by."

"No. We won't. I got lots of wires out—we'll have all the men an' firepower we need if even half of them show up."

"Who you wire?"

"Dirty Eddie, Snaker Ray, Li'l Tommy, Mick, Big Elk—a bunch of men who'd do us the most good. I offered good money."

"Eddie—he's *morte*, no?"

"No—that was his brother the Pinkertons got."

"Ees good. I always like Dirty Eddie."

There's a thing about living as an outlaw an' gunslinger. None of us ever ask another what his last name may be. Arm an' me, we didn't have the reputations most of the others did, so we didn't care. But a good percentage of the outlaws have range names—like Snaker Ray an' Dirty Eddie. Boys like the Earps played on both sides of the law and didn't give a damn who knew their names. Billy the Kid was as crazy as a shithouse rat an' went by Bill Bonney as much as anything else. The James brothers were too well-known for range names—and too arrogant to use them, anyway.

The men I wired were hard cases Arm and I had come across and spent time with—usually in various criminal activities. They trusted us; we trusted them.

"The ladies," Arm said, "have stew an' biscuits for us. You are hongry?"

"You bet."

Teresa an' Blanca had a big pot of venison stew simmering, and the scent of it was enough to carry a man off. Plus, there were biscuits that might well have floated off, they were so light and warm—and a huge bowl of mashed potatoes and a dish of canned tomatoes an' so forth.

I ate like a starving sow and so did Arm. It's strange how men like us see death. Gunslingers an' bank robbers an' such almost inevitably die in a fight or during a robbery. Some are grabbed up by the Pinkertons an' are hung. Others would simply screw up an' sit with their backs to a window.

Tiny was different, and he deserved a lot more than me or Arm meeting one man in a gunfight. Tiny was a good man—a genuinely good man— which is the sort of fella not many of us knew. Me an Arm got lucky—he was our friend—our good friend.

I knew as soon as I saw Tiny's bullet-riddled body that I'd face Dansworth. There was no question about that. Not only would I face him, but I'd kill him and watch his eyes as he died. I'd take that beautiful .45 of his and use it as my own. Each time I drew it I'd remember Tiny an' how Dansworth died with my bullets in him.

See, that's how lots of us lived during those times.

We decided that we'd never leave the barn un-guarded. Tiny had boarded up Blanca an' Teresa's windows with some of the lumber he had left over from his working on the barn. We tol' them to stay on the floor if trouble started. Tiny said the Sharps wouldn't make it through the lumber—it was fresh and hard—so we tried it out. All of us—the ladies, Arm, and me—stood out by the barn. I loaded up the Sharps, bored a clean hole through timber across the window, and blew the slug out through the back wall. The sumbitch might still be goin', as far as I know.

"We stay floor," Blanca said.

The weather screws around as it generally does in West Texas spring. We'd have days that were so intensely and perfectly salubrious—a word M. Chambery taught me in fourth grade, the year I dropped out—that we never wanted them to end. Other days—even the ones following the great ones—must have been hangovers from February, with cruel, biting winds and even snow.

The animals were fractious because of being confined in stalls so much, but Arm an' me didn't dare let them out into the corral or pasture with only the pair of us to guard them.

Our stud turned ornery, climbing an' striking an' being miserable. He ate, but that's all he did right. We had to board his stall higher and make the gate and front stouter with three-quarter-inch planks.

The foal was looking real good, but he was restless and bored. When he thought it'd be fun to nip his teeth 'round his ma's nipples, she spun, knocked him off his feet, and chewed a tiny patch of hide off his flank. He squealed like a scalded cat—but apparently figured out that just sucking was the way to go.

The Appy colt had not a problem in the world. Arm had given him a pig bladder to play with. He'd done the same with our own colt, but he showed no interest at all. The Ap, though, nosed and shoved that bladder around his stall, as happy as a kid at a county fair with a pocketful of pennies.

"That colt, when he is older, might throw a better foal'n our mare's done," Arm said, as we stood there watching the Ap play with the bladder.

I hated to admit it, but I said, "He's got all the personality he needs. He's put together good, too."

"Good? The Appy, he's damn near perfect, no? Lookit his chest, his forelegs, lookit how he handles himself. Damn, Jake . . ."

I didn't argue.

The first of our crew rode in about two weeks later. He was called "One Foot," for obvious reasons. Union canister shot had taken of his heel at Second Bull Run and the surgeons lopped off the rest. He wasn't what you'd call a pleasant fella. His first words were, "What're you payin'?"

"What do you want?" I asked.

"A thousand."

"We'll pay you two, you do what we need you to do."

He thought that over. "You need ears or scalps or noses or peckers?"

"Nope."

"You got a deal. Hacking stuff off men I've killed never made no sense to me. If I say I killed 'em, then I killed 'em."•

Dirty Eddie showed up next and he an' Arm embraced like a pair of brothers. Eddie was somewhat strange-looking: he had scalps acrossed his chest an' back, strung on latigo, and he was near goddam a one-man munitions dump. He carried four .45s—two in left an' right holsters, an' two in cross-draw shoulder holsters. There was a 30.30 in each side of his saddle at his knees and behind him on the cantle. The heft of a pair of Bowies showed at his boot tops, an' anyone who thought he wasn't carryin' at least a pair of Derringers was a damned fool.

Three Pinkertons thought they had him just outside of Dodge a couple years ago. They're pushin' up daisies now—they thought they'd stripped him of weapons. They were wrong.

A gent named Mad Dog—half Paiute, half Mexican, and all crazy—jogged in on a thoroughbred horse he'd stolen way the hell off in Kentucky. We put up the horses as men dribbled in. They spread their trail blankets wherever they cared to—in the living room, in the barn, and in the kitchen. After another week or so we had ten men and we figured that was plenty. Most knew one another, but there was little chitchat or catching up. These guys weren't big on talking.

Blanca an' Teresa shagged the kitchen sleepers out early in the morning and prepared huge breakfasts, probably more than most of the men would eat in the course of an average day.

The ladies didn't much care for our troops. They were afraid of them, seeing them as partners with Satan. "To keel for money is a great sin," Blanca said.

During the day the men hung around, playing poker, drinking, and riding our land. One or two would ride into town every so often, but encountered little trouble. It was apparent to Dansworth that we'd brought in help; he had riders posted all around our farm.

One observer rode into rifle range and that was a big mistake. Dirty Eddie picked him off and then rode out to see if he had anything worth taking. "His horse was a joke—wormy, underfed, missing a shoe. I unsaddled him an' sent him on his way. The rider's .45 was missing one of its grips and was rusted to boot." He held up a bottle of cheap whiskey. "This was all that was worth taking," he said. "His saddle was held together with spit an' baling twine. If these are the sort of men we're after, a battle ain't gonna take long."

I didn't have an actual plan an' I called all the men together at lunchtime a week or so after they'd arrived. "They hang in that one saloon," I said, "but they're generally all around town, too—the general store, restaurant, and so forth."

"Well, hell," a fella named Chester said, "that don't seem to present no problem. Why not just ride in an' shoot their asses off an' git this thing finished up?"

No one—including Arm an' me—had any problems with that plan. It'd be quick, clean, and would solve our problem in a big hurry.

"We'll need at least a couple of men to stay an' watch over the horses," I said. "An' one other thing: I want Dansworth. Leave him standing. You'll recognize him by his fancy clothes an' polished boots. It's personal between him an' me."

"I hear-tell he's handy with that Colt of his," Dirty Eddie said.

"Maybe. I guess I'll find out."

Deciding who'd stay to watch the horses an' farm took considerable debate, much of it loud an' profane, bordering on gunfights.

"Look," I yelled over the clamor, "we'll each write our names on a little piece of paper. The one drawn stays. I'll pay him extra. The rest of us ride."

"Who holds the papers?"

"I'll ask one of our ladies," I said. "Fair enough?"

"We gotta see the names go in the hat."

"Jesus. Yeah. You'll see that. I got a piece of foolscap from the desk in the living room and tore it into a dozen fairly even pieces. I gave one to each man. They passed a nub of a pencil around.

"I dunno how to write," someone pointed out.

"Then give the paper to somebody else to write your name on. Or draw a goddamn picture or make a mark."

Then I went up to get Blanca, while our troops sucked away at our liquor supply.

"There's no danger—all they'll do is choose a

slip of paper from a hat, Blanca. There's nothin' to be afraid of."

"Is always good to fear Satan."

"They're not Satan—they're jus' men, like me an' like Arm."

"No es verdad."

"It *is* true, Blanca—they're a little scruffy, and they live different than most people, but they ain't devils."

"They are loco keelers."

"But . . . but . . . see, Blanca . . . they live differently. They don't . . ."

"Ees boolsheet." I'd never heard her use any language the pope wouldn't use. She put her hand on my arm. "I weel do it. Is good? No? But, I weel play a game with the devil."

"I don't . . ."

"Hush now," Blanca demanded. "We go now an' do the sleeps of paper. You an' Armando have been good to us. I can do this—but I no owe you my holy an' 'ternal soul, ya know? This is one time, is all. I can go to 'fession soon. But when I draw the sleep I pray in my head."

"Fine. Okay. Thanks, Blanca."

The men were sitting and standing around as I'd left them. "Wait a minnit," a guy named Lefty snarled. "Who's goin' to be holdin' the papers?"

This was getting tiresome. "Look," I said, "we'll put 'em in a hat an' blindfold Blanca. Now—let's cut the horseshit an' get to it."

I pushed the slips off the table into my hat and shook hell outta them. Arm tied his bandana around Blanca's head, completely covering her eyes. I took Blanca's hand an' held it over my inverted hat. "All you gotta do is pick one," I said.

Blanca put her hand into the hat as if she were sticking it in a box of scorpions. She plucked out one slip. I took the paper and showed it around. "Looks like Lou is stayin'," I said. "The rest of us will ride out after dark."

"I din't ride here to set in a goddamn barn," Lou said. "Suppose you or the Mex got drawed? Would you hang back?"

I suppose I answered louder and more hostile than I needed to. "I'm tired of this shit. Arm an' me are runnin' this show—the ones who pay the money an' give the orders. If that bothers any of you, saddle up an' get the hell off our land."

"Feisty today, ain't he?" Dirty Eddie said.

"I'll show you how feisty I am tonight, when we get to Hulberton," I said.

"You got some kinda plan, Jake?" Mad Dog asked. "Or are we jist gonna charge in an' shoot hell outta everybody an' everything?"

Mad Dog gave me a quick shiver, and for a moment I thought that Blanca's satanic theory just might be right. Dog didn't care which way it went. He'd just as soon kill women an' kids as gunfighters an' lawmen. It was all the same to him.

"I see anybody take down a civilian," I said, sweeping my eyes over the crew, "I'll shoot him off his horse right there—no questions asked, no explanations accepted. Arm will do the same thing. Clear?" Some of the men nodded. No one said anything. It seemed like I might have said nothing more important than, "The punkin crop looks good this year."

"I ain't Quantrill," I said, "an' Hulberton ain't Lawrence, out in Kansas. We go right for the saloon—me an' Arm will lead—an' engage the sonsabitches inside an' outside the place."

Mad Dog smirked at the word "engage."

"One other thing," I said. "Anybody hit bad enough to be shot off his horse—well—it's up to him what happens to him. Most likely, he'll get his ass shot off. Point is, we're not bringing any wounded back here to croak. Minor wounds where a man can still ride an' shoot, they ride back with us. We don't want hostages or prisoners. We're not carryin' any of Dansworth's men anywhere but to hell."

I figured the best way to come in would be in a mass—there was no sense botherin' with half the boys from one side an' half from the other. This was gonna be like Pickett's charge in that town in Pennsylvania—Gettysburg—an' battle plans would be useless. It'd be a matter of killing or being killed.

I tried to re-befriend my stallion for a good part of the rest of the day, but he wasn't having any part of it. I couldn't approach him without him rearing and baring his teeth, no matter what kinda treat I brought or how I sweet-talked him. I shouldn't have tried to ride him. He was as wild as a hawk an' everything had been going good. It'd take some time to gain back the ground I'd lost, and it was a sure thing I'd never again drop a saddle over the ornery sumbitch.

Some of the crew slept. Others played poker

and finished off Arm's and my booze supply. There was some gunfire, but not a real lot of it. These men knew their weapons better'n they knew their horses or anything or anyone else in their lives. A few checked out their rifles. A long ride in a saddle scabbard could tick a sight off a hair. All of us knew, though, that we wouldn't be shooting from any distance, so a tiny vacillation didn't mean anything.

Teresa an' Blanca fed us their usual wondrous meal and an extra big pot of their coffee. Lots of coffee—particularly range and cattle-drive coffee—is weak an' hardly worth drinking. 'Hands dump it down, because that's all there is. But the coffee at the Busted Thumb Horse Ranch brought smiles to the faces of all the men. It was strong enough to melt a horseshoe, had none of that goddamn chicory in it, and always had a taste of the Mex coffee that had the power of a cannon, but was never bitter.

We saddled up as the sun was on the verge of the horizon. The moon was about half and threw some light because there were few clouds. The horses hadn't been ridden in a group and there was some squealing and biting, but nothing serious. We rode out, Arm an' me side by side, in front, headed for Hulberton.

We rode at a lope, not pushing our animals, and not afraid of the noise the herd of us were making. Dansworth knew we'd be coming sometime. He had a few lookouts posted outside of town. Somebody shot one off his horse, and the other two or three hauled ass to town. Mad Dog picked off one of them.

There were a pair of big freighter wagons loaded with barrels of beer maybe a hundred feet apart in front of the saloon. As soon as the surviving outlooks pulled in, the freighters moved ahead, face-to-face, making decent cover. Rifle fire at us started as soon as the freighters were moved, men shooting from between the barrels.

It became immediately obvious I'd wired the right lunatics. They answered the rifle fire muzzle flashes with their own 30.30s—from horseback, mind you—and picked off maybe six or seven of the men who thought they had cover.

A flood of men and gunfire poured out of the saloon—and most of them dropped as soon as they appeared. Mad Dog swung in close on that thoroughbred of his, picking his shots with his .45. He was doing a lot of damage when he ran his horse into shotgun range and went down. It was messy—he and his animal must have gotten both barrels of a twelve gauge. Mad Dog got a good part of his face blown off and was dead immediately. His horse was trying to suck air through a throat that was gushing blood and he, too, died in a few moments.

I swung my horse back hard—almost running into one of my own men—because I saw the shotgun man reloading. I put two rounds in his midbody and one in his head.

I heard glass shattering over the gunfire and saw Dirty Eddie's horse ground-tied in front of the general store. I wasn't sure what he was doing, but I had to swing back or make an easy target.

Arm was riding in too close, but he was low on his horse, and he was dropping Dansworth's men very handily. I saw him plug a rifleman and figured Arm knew what he was doing.

More and more men started shooting from behind the freighters and from the saloon. One of our men went down—and then another.

"Head home!" I bellowed. "Head home now!"

Heavy gunfire followed us as we galloped out of Hulberton, but it was little more than noise. None of the remaining crew was hit. Dirty Eddie had a pair of large canvas sacks riding in front of him, and he was sucking on a bottle of booze. I slowed a tad.

"What the hell, Eddie?"

"Whiskey an' tobacco." He grinned.

Arm an' me led the crew back toward our ranch. I turned in my saddle a couple of times to check our losses, but clouds had moved in and it was hard to see—particularly since the guys were strung out in a ragged line with some yards between them, rather than riding in a cluster. We didn't ride hard, but we kept moving at a fast lope.

None of Dansworth's army was chasing us, which told me they were as disorganized and stupid as I thought they were. We were way the hell outnumbered, and even losers like Dansworth's men could have done us some damage.

I was starting to feel pretty good about our sneak attack—our raid—and I looked back over my shoulder to see where Dirty Eddie was with his supply of booze. A sip or so woulda gone down nice. The clouds shifted a hair and I caught a glint of moonlight on a bottle Eddie was sucking on. I raised my arm to bring him up to me an' Arm.

That's when things went straight to hell.

For a tiny bit of a second it looked to me like one of our men dove from his horse. Then I heard the deep thud of a Sharps. Immediately following that there was a searing burst of pure white light—like lightning on a dark night. The blast was a totally, impossibly loud roar. Those of us who'd been in the war had learned to hate and fear that weapon—a goddamn small artillery cannon firing canister shot.

I'd heard somewheres that the Union developed canister, but I know the rebs used it, too. The load looked like a large tin can—like a two-quart peach can. It was filled with minié balls and pieces of metal—U-shaped with each edge surface razor sharp—and black powder. When minié balts and metal were short, the cans were loaded with horseshoe nails, pebbles, and whatever bits of steel or other metal could be found. A well-placed canister round could take down—tear apart—twenty men or more, depending on how they were positioned.

Canister was what made it possible to walk across the several acres of Seminary Ridge—Pickett's charge—stepping only on dead rebs. The little stream to the east of the stone wall held by the Union ran with blood—it didn't appear to be water at all, just blood.

There weren't any options except to take out the artillery and hope they didn't have another. Our boys were shooting at muzzle flashes of rifles and were taking down men, but that cannon . . .

I figured this was my show—mine and Arm's—and it was up to me to do something. I slid my Sharps out of its scabbard and swung to the left of the cannon. Then, I buried my heels in my horse's sides and raced at the artillery piece, reins in my teeth, Sharps to my shoulder, ready to fire. Since I was off to the side of the main battle I wasn't noticed right away.

In the meager light of the torch man at the cannon I saw what I was looking for—a small wooden barrel. Firing from a galloping horse in full darkness isn't what one might call easy—or even sane. But, like I said, I had no options.

Dansworth's men didn't notice me coming on until I was seventy-five or so yards out. Hell, that's spittin' distance for my rifle, but distance wasn't the problem, accuracy was. I aimed as well as I could and squeezed off my shot. It seemed like I'd barely touched the trigger when there was a detonation that would make the July sun look like a firefly. Everything lit up for maybe twenty yards around where the little barrel had stood. I could clearly see dead men—and pieces of dead men—and the sky was raining all kinds of crap. An arm dropped directly in front of us, scaring my horse (an' me) as I swung hard back the way I'd come. A small wheel slammed into the ground to my side and a spatter of tortured chunks and lengths of steel were striking the ground all over the place.

So much for the cannon. I just hoped that they didn't have another.

I got back to my boys and we headed home without resistance. That explosion was something, all right—I couldn't hear and I don't think the others could, either. Arm touched my shoulder and said something, but all I saw was his mouth moving.

My men had no particular allegiance to one another. They were here for the money primarily, and secondarily because Arm an' me had helped them in some major fashion. Nobody said much, either, because they couldn't hear yet, or because they knew four of their comrades, friends or not, had been killed.

I got out bottles of liniment and we all rubbed down our horses' legs—we'd given them some hard run. Then we used sacks to sweep the sweat off their chests and rear quarters. We gave water slowly—the animals were hot an' tired and sucking too much cold water would go right to their hooves and initiate founder—a swelling inside the hoof that disabled a horse, permanently, very frequently.

A couple of the guys had relatively superficial wounds, lacerations we could use horse liniment on an' then wrap. Arm's horse had a gouge across his rump from a bullet, but it wasn't deep. A couple of other of the animals had been hit as well, but there was nothing too serious.

Dirty Eddie passed out whiskey, tobacco, and papers as we worked on our horses. He'd grabbed nine quarts and only two had broken, because he stuffed sacks of Bull D'urham between the bottles.

When we'd turned our horses into stalls, we sat on bales of hay and got to drinkin'. "That cannon," Eddie said, "coulda beat us easily 'nuff, 'cept for Jake blowin' their keg."

"They could have another one—or more," someone offered.

"It's a right sure bet them men aren't goin' to sit

tight. They're gonna attack us here, just like we did at their saloon."

"They loss many men," Arm said.

"Yeah," I said, "but they got plenty more. I don't see no way we can get more troops in here in time to save our asses."

Dirty Eddie lowered his bottle. "I do," he said. "I know this ol' battle scavenger who's got a ton of weapons he picked up after battles."

"We use to shoot them sonsabitches," one of the men said. "They took wallets an' pitchers an' them Catholic beads . . ."

"Rosaries," I said.

"Yeah. Them. An' belts an' boots an' medals an' surgeon's tools from medics who got shot down."

"That ain't the point," Eddie said. "He might have a cannon or two or other stuff we could use."

"Where's he live?" I asked.

"Not more'n a couple days from here, if I recollect right. Some of it's hard ridin' but we'd make it."

"An' carry the cannon on horseback? Makes no sense. We need to take our women's wagon."

There was a silence that lasted for a long time while men drank whiskey and thought about the possible cache of weapons.

"How do we know this scavenger's got anything we want?"

Dirty Eddie grinned. "We don't. Seems to me it's worth a try, though. He could even have dynamite. If he don't have nothin', we can kill him anyway. Jake? Wadda you thinkin'?"

"I dunno. We'd need to have men away from the ranch for a couple days, an' we lost four men tonight. That'll leave but five to stay here an' fight if Dansworth attacks. The odds ain't good."

"The odds in Hulberton, they were no good, either. An' we kill what? Maybe seven or eight to each of their men for every one of ours—maybe more. We can no theenk of odds, Jake."

I thought that over. Arm was right. "Okay," I said, "me an' Eddie will go out at first light tomorrow with the wagon an' well make the ride without stopping. We should be back in a day an' a half. Arm, you gotta run the show here."

"*Sí. No problema*."

The men looked around at one another. "Seems like we ain't got no choice," one said. "Gimme that bottle."

The one thing we didn't need at all was rain, an' 'course that's what we got. It started pourin' down like the sky busted open a bit after midnight. By false dawn, it'd tapered off to a constant, soaking drizzle that turned the ground to mud.

"Roads are gonna be a damn mess," I said to Eddie as we harnessed the horse in front of the cart.

"Don't matter. We ain't gonna be on roads anyhow."

We pulled out long before full light, wrapped in our dusters with our canvas ponchos over them, with a bottle of whiskey an' some food Teresa an' Blanca had put up for us.

We'd tightened the horses' shoes and they

didn't seem to be having too much trouble hauling the wagon, although the mud sucked at their hooves and the wagon wheels, making the trip tougher on them. Eddie began tapping at the bottle 'fore we were outta sight of the barn. I saw no reason not to join him.

It wasn't that the temperature was real low; that wasn't the problem. What bothered us was the constant spatter of the rain and the goddamn wetness of everything.

"Tell me about this fella we're goin' to see," I said.

"Sumbith was a profiteer, sellin' ammo an' whatever else to both sides. 'Course when he sold out his stock, he had a empty wagon or two an' that's what he an' his men would fill with whatever they could find at battle sites—rifles, clothes, black powder, swords, small artillery pieces, all that kinda thing. Also, they damned near stripped the dead: boots, Bibles, letters, whatever-the-hell. Then they'd haul ass back to his place an' stash their loot in his barn. Sonsabitches cleaned up at Second Bull Run an' at Gettysburg, an' lots of smaller skirmishes, too. They done their stealin' at night. Either the rebs or the Yanks managed to kill a half dozen or so of them, but the main man—name of Hargis—always managed to get clear." He was silent for a moment. "Dirty business, robbin' the dead like that. It ain't right."

"Yeah," I agreed.

"I gotta tell you this," Dirty Eddie said, "I'm gonna kill him. I been meanin' to for some time. Should we find him, I'll shoot him."

"Fine with me," I said.

The horses struggled some on slopes that wouldn't have slowed them, 'cept for the mud. We rested an' watered them often. There sure was no shortage of water—their were foot-deep puddles in every little depression.

The rain finally let up about dusk. The sky cleared. "I know the stars fairly good," Eddie said. "I went to sea once when I was a kid runnin' from a murder charge. No reason we can't keep right on goin'.'"

I nodded. I planned on that anyway.

We'd gone through our whiskey by the time the rain stopped. A little breeze came up, puttin' a wet chill on everythin'.

"I wouldn't say no to another taste of whiskey," I said.

Eddie grinned and pulled a fresh bottle out from under the seat, where he'd packed it up in straw. "I believe I'll join you," he said.

We rode along for a couple of hours, Eddie every so often craning his neck and looking up at the sky, a couple of times drawing an arc in the air with his finger. I noticed he was clean shaven—even under his chin an' neck where it's hard to get the whiskers, and that his poncho was cleaner than mine. His hat—a Stetson, of course— was snugged down low over his eyebrows and the hat, too, was in far finer condition than mine.

"Care to answer a question, Eddie?" I asked.

"I'm innocent. I didn't do it. I wasn't nowhere near the place." His teeth were white in the moonlight as he smiled.

"No, no—it's not that type of question."

"Well, have at it, Jake," he said.

"See, ever since I've knowed you, I've called you Dirty Eddie, and so have all the other men like us. Thing is, there's nothing dirty about you. You shave, you lop off your hair when it needs it, you wear decent clothes an' good boots—so what the hell?"

Eddie laughed. "I thought everybody knew that story." He rolled a smoke and lit it. "I wasn't but a young sprout—maybe sixteen, seventeen—an' I'd taken a shine to the sister of three brothers who were real tough boys. They warned me off but, 'course, I didn't pay no attention. One night I climbed up a trellis to the gal's room an' I was havin' my way with her, when don't one of her brothers bust in, all ready to wring my neck like a Sunday chicken. I went out the window without my pants or boots or gun belt, busted the trellis climbin' down, an' looked for a place to hide. All these folks had was a few hundred acres of wheat, an' it wasn't more'n a few inches high at that time a year. By then, I could hear all three of them brothers clamberin' down the stairs. Well, hell. They'da pounded me inta the ground—an' probably killed me. Then I seen the privy. I ran over to it an' shoved my way under the back an' into the pit an' stood there in shit an' piss all that night an' into the morning. When them boys mounted up at first light, each carryin' a twelve gauge, I gave 'em a good amount of time an' then climbed out of the pit an' ran my ass off to a friend of mine's place—a blacksmith. He gimme some clothes an' a pair of raggedy-ass boots an' a horse an' I left that county in a hurry. But he laughed so hard I thought he'd bust wide-open.

This smith, he liked to run his mouth, an' he give me the name Dirty Eddie, ever time he told the story. An' that's who I been nigh unto twenty-five years."

"Don't it bother you?"

"Nah."

"Did you ever come across those brothers?"

"Yeah. I killed one in Tombstone. He tried to draw on me. I dunno 'bout the other two, but I don't lose no sleep over 'em."

I drifted off after Eddie's story. We were on fairly level ground an' the wagon was moving well. The horses were okay. We fed them oats we'd brought along an' gave them some rest.

When we started up again, the sun was doin' its best to make a appearance, an' finally it did. Me an' Dirty Eddie shed our ponchos in a hurry, an' after another hour, our dusters. The sun was flexing its muscles. At first, 'course, it felt real fine—an' then it turned into heat. We had to drink outta the shrinking puddles, 'cause neither of us had been bright 'nuff to fill a couple canteens. I always liked the taste of rainwater from a clean puddle, so it didn't bother me.

We'd long since finished the sliced venison an' biscuits the ladies had sent along an' both of us were damned near starved.

"We might best park these horses an' look around for game. I'm so goddamn hungry I could eat a boot," Eddie said. "I don't give a damn— prairie dog, snake, whatever-the-hell."

"Let's do it, then." I was driving an' I reined in. We tied the horses to the weight the ladies carried—they didn't like hitchin' posts—and Eddie went one way an' me another.

It was hot an' walkin' wasn't much fun, bein' hungover an' hungry. I loosened my Colt in my holster a bit—the dampness had tightened the leather a hair—an' walked on out. After about a thousand miles, I figured it was a lost cause. I hadn't seen a prairie dog or anything else. I drew on a sidewinder but he scooted into a bunch of rocks. I kicked some stone around, but he musta had a good den an' I wasn't about to go diggin' for him. There was no size to him anyway— maybe three feet.

I didn't see no sense in trekkin' out farther, hoping Dirty Eddie had bagged something. If not—well, hell—both of us had been hungry before.

Then I got real lucky. I was scuffin' along, not real payin' attention to the terrain like I should, when I heard the beating and flurry of wings. Five or six prairie hens went up in a cluster of noise an' dust. I dropped four of them and missed the others. I walked to the little buncha weeds they were in an' found seven eggs. I grabbed up the hens, pocketed the eggs in my vest an' shirt, an' went back to the wagon.

Eddie already had a fire going. He was skinning out three rattlers, not one of them big enough to make a meal. He flung the snakes over his shoulder when he saw the feast I'd brought.

We didn't have a pan to fry the eggs in, so after we stripped down the birds, we broke the eggs over the birds as they cooked.

The scent of them hens cooking was as sweet as a young chicken on a spit at a picnic, an' they tasted at least as good. We pulled them offa the sticks an' gnawed away at that sweet meat. Dirty Eddie an' me ate all four of the hens an' sucked the marrow outta the big bones.

"We ain't far now," Eddie said. "Let's move on. If I'm right, over them next two rises is Hargis's place."

We topped the first rise and saw nothing. The second climb we stopped an' looked down at what Dirty Eddie said was a war-scavanger's cache.

Chapter Nine

It seemed like we'd been rolling forever. "You sure you know where we're going?" I asked Eddie.

"Yep. The stars don't lie."

"Well, look. My ass is numb, I need a drink, an' it's too damn cold out here."

"You're gonna make me cry," Dirty Eddie said.

After a bit, I asked, "Why do you want to kill this Hargis fella? I don't doubt that he needs killin'—robbin' our boys like that an' then makin' a profit—but why *you?*"

I expected a "Why not me?" sort of response, but that isn't what I got.

Eddie rolled himself a smoke and lit it. "See, I had a what?—half cousin or so goddamn thing—but I spent lots of time with the kid before I had to start runnin' from the law. His name was Uriah. We fished an' hunted. His pa was a mean drunk—beat hell outta Uriah an' Uriah's ma when he had a load on. I was but fifteen or sixteen an' not real big, an' I knew I couldn't take him when he was sober. So, I waited out in their barn 'til I heard Uriah's ma scream an' a bunch of crashin' around in the house. I had me a ax handle an' I went on into the house an' beat hell outta that mean ol' bastard. Thing is, I killed him—busted his head open."

He flicked the nub of his smoke into a puddle.

"Me an' Uriah, we planted his pa way the hell out in their wheat field, an' figured that was the end of it. It weren't. Uriah's ma went to the sheriff an' accused me of murder an' said she seen me kill her husband, which she did. So, I had to scramble."

"I see. But Hargis . . ."

"Uriah, he joined on with the Confederacy, like any good Texan would. He caught a Union minié ball 'twixt his eyes at Antioch. I heard about that an' went on out there, plannin' to ship him home an' plant him on his own ground. I talked to some of the wounded rebs an' learned Hargis got to Uriah real quick—took his boots an' rifle an' sidearm. Thing is, Uriah, he had a ring his gramma give him when he was a kid an' Hargis couldn't get the ring off, so he took the finger. That's when I decided to kill Hargis—an' that's what I'll do. But the goddamn law an' the Pinkertons an' the bounty hunters been chasin' me like a hound after a bitch in heat, an' I ain't had a chance. Seems like I got one now."

"Well," I said.

Dirty Eddie nodded. "I figured you'd understand or I wouldna run my yap."

"Don't make my ass less numb or me less cold if you kill or don't kill this ghoul."

"Wassa a ghoul?"

"Kinda ghost or spirit that come back to life an' screws about with livin' people."

"Oh."

We started up a gentle rise, the horses working well, the wagon wheels making good purchase, even through the slop. We reined in at the top of the rise.

"There she is," Dirty Eddie said. "Din't I tell you the stars don' lie?"

We sat there an' let the horses blow an' looked over the place. It wasn't a farm—there was nothing plowed an' nothing growing we could see in the murky light, but there was a small corral for horses.

The barn was way the hell bigger than it needed to be for a farm that didn't grow nothing. And, I never seen three men with rifles guarding a barn that shoulda been empty.

We were maybe 400 to 450 yards from the barn. "Maybe could be your buffalo gun could take out that fella leanin' 'gainst the front doors," Eddie said. He spoke as if my rifle—or me—couldn't make the shot.

I unwrapped my rifle from its deerskin. "Sounds like you're looking for a bet, Eddie. How about a case of good whiskey?"

"How about two?" He grinned.

"You're on."

The damn fool at the front of the barn scratched a match to light a smoke. It was like shooting a elephant from six foot away. I loaded up, aimed, and carved a hole in the man's chest the size of a dinner plate.

"Nice. I can't reach out near that far with a 30.30. Care to keep shooting?"

"Sure."

"No more bets, though."

These scavengers were scum—no better'n men who diddled li'l kids. I had no more feelin' for them that I did when I was target shootin'.

"Lookit there," Dirty Eddie said.

One of the men was behind a water trough and he had his hat either on a stick or the barrel of his sidearm, and was moving it back an' forth. I laughed an' so did Eddie.

"Clever trick, no?" I said.

"Fooled hell outta me," Eddie said.

The thumb-size .44-caliber slug from my rifle would blow through that trough like it were a birthday cake—and through the barn, as well, an' still kill a man a couple hundred yards beyond the barn.

"Question is," Eddie said, grinning, "is that jasper in front of the hat or behind it?"

"Another bet?"

"I need odds. Two to one."

"Yer ass."

"Okay, okay, even odds—a case. Take your shot, Jake."

My thought was that the scavenger was leading with the hat an' backing up an' then goin' forward an' then back again, an' so forth. I loaded my rifle. When the hat reached about half trough, I squeezed off a round. The impact flung the fella's body up an' into the side of the barn; then he dropped to the ground.

"Lucky shot," Dirty Eddie growled.

"Lucky or not, I won't have to buy booze for a while."

The third guard was at the hayloft of the barn, gawkin' out, tryin' to figure out what to do. I took him through the thick lumber of the hayloft opening.

"Let's go on down," Eddie said. "Hargis is sneakin' around somewheres, but he ain't got the balls to face either one of us."

We kinda angled down the slope to keep the wagon from skiddin' an' spookin' the horses an' pulled up in front of the barn. Eddie drove down; I rewrapped my Sharps.

"What're you boys after?" a voice called from inside the barn. "You can take whatever you want—no need to shoot me. Hell, I got a little cash I can give you, too."

"You Hargis?"

"Yessir—at your service. I got guns, sabers, boots, all kinds of—"

"Slide the door open," Eddie said.

Hargis did so. He was a fat man—as broad as a beer barrel and without no more muscle than a maggot. Hell, if someone were to hang him, he wouldn't know what chin to put the noose around.

"Go 'round an' light some lanterns," Eddie said. "An' 'member there're two guns on you an' neither one of us have missed in a long time. Ask your three men, you don't believe me."

Hargis scurried the way really fat men do—tryin' to move fast but held back by his body, so his motions were jerky, uncoordinated. He lit a half dozen lanterns hangin' from beams the length of the barn. Eddie an' me climbed down an' walked inside.

It kinda made me sick. Hargis had more muskets than the Rhode Island militia, two long tables of percussion pistols an' some revolvers, a big pile of boots an' gloves, an' what looked to be fifty or more swords an' sabers hung on the wall. There was another long table like you'd see in a mercantile covered with books, Bibles, diaries, pictures, an' so forth—the personal stuff the boys carried. There were lots of pocket watches an' lockets.

Along on side of the barn were five small artillery pieces, such as like Dansworth had tried on us. There was a small stack of sacks of black powder. There were a few military saddles, some bits an' bridles, and sets of reins. At the far end of the barn, still in the half dark, was a small two-wheeled wagon with somethin' on it covered by a big tarp.

"What's that down there?" I asked.

"Jus' miscellaneous crap we picked up," Hargis said.

"You got any rings?" Dirty Eddie asked.

Hargis grinned a fat-man grin. "Sure—whole box of 'em right over here." He led us to the other side of the barn an' pointed to a trunk. Eddie hefted its sides an' upended it, spilling what seemed like all the rings in the world onto the floor. Hargis's mouth opened to say something, but then he closed it. Eddie swept his hands through the rings, spreading them out. Lots of them had small stones, and lots had initials or symbols of the Union or the Confederacy on them.

It took a good while for Dirty Eddie to find what he was after. When he did, he held it reverently, like it were a holy object. "Where'd you git this?" he asked.

"That there is a fine piece," Hargis said. "Real fine. I bought it from a Rebel officer who was down on his luck an' had lost all his money in a poker—"

Eddie didn't stand from his crouch over the rings, but his draw was fast and smooth. He emptied his .45 into the fat man. Eddie put the ring in his pocket. "Let's see what's on the cart," he said.

He walked down the length of the barn, feeling as if we were walking through a cemetery of unburied corpses.

We approached the cart, me on one side and Eddie on the other, and dragged off the tarp.

"Holy God," Eddie said.

"I didn't think . . . Jesus, man . . ." was all I could get out.

"Let's cover it up an' roll, Jake."

"Sure," I said. "Yeah. Let's do that. We can use Hargis's horses; it isn't that big and doesn't weigh that much."

Eddie stood as if in a daze. "Ya know, I done a bunch a battles in the war an I ain't I never seen one them things. Sure did hear 'bout 'em, though."

"Let's get it back to the ranch. Dansworth ain't gonna waste much time screwin' around—he wants them horses real bad—an' he wants to kill us real bad."

Eddie looked over the cart. "Let's tie this baby down an' grab one of Hargis's nags to pull it. We'll tie our horses on the back—they done good work gettin' us here."

"Let's take a look in the house—maybe find some grub," I said.

We didn't find much food, but there was a good

supply of corn liquor. We loaded a few bottles on the cart and kept one with us as we set off back to the Busted Thumb.

The ground had dried out some an' the two horses we took were decent animals, willing to pull. We drank corn and talked. "This sumbitch is gonna be a big surprise to Dansworth," Eddie said. "Jus' like that artillery piece was to us."

"You ever operate one?"

"No."

"Can't be too hard," I said. "Doesn't seem like there's a lot to it."

"I guess we'll find out," Eddie said, " 'cause we ain't got time to screw around with it now. What we gotta do is get back." He jigged the horses a bit and they picked up their pace. Eddie grinned. "I'm gonna rub these boys down real good back at the ranch, an' purely feed hell out of 'em with that molasses grain."

We got back about dinnertime, which was good, 'cause we were damn near starved. We drove the cart right on into the barn. Arm had been riding guard an' he seen us an' rode in with us.

"Any action?" I asked.

"No. Nothing. Ain't gonna be long, though. They'll come at night, no?"

"That's the way I'd do it."

We faced the cart out and left the tarp on it. A few of the boys peeked and walked away grinning and shaking their heads like they couldn't quite believe what they'd just seen.

At Teresa an' Blanca's great dinner, we discussed what few plans we had.

"They're sure as hell gonna torch the house," one of the boys said. "We'd best bring the ladies into the barn with the rest of us, 'cept for a couple outriders to give us a alarm."

"*Sí*. They'll no burn the barn 'cause that's where the mare an' foal are."

"All we gotta do is shoot them down an' the game is over," someone said. "This corn whiskey tastes like sidewinder piss," he added.

"Be plenty *dineros* for you men for good whiskey when theese is over."

Nothing much happened that night. A couple of riders—staying way the hell outta range—come by to look things over, but that was about it.

It was strange how calm our men were. They played cards, slept, cleaned and lubricated their weapons, and drank corn. Maybe when a fella has been in so many battles, put his life on the line so many times, it becomes no more than a job—like a ribbon clerk goin' to work in the mornin' in a mercantile. Even as the day dragged on, the tension level stayed low an' easy.

"Ain't you boys afraid of nothin'?" I asked Dirty Eddie.

He pondered for a few moments. "Well, I never been partial to scorpions," he said. "I always shake out my boots real good 'fore I put 'em on."

"About fightin'," I mean.

"Fightin'? Naw. What's to be scared of? We'll either get killed or not get killed. We all know a bullet's gonna catch us one day, but what day that it is don't matter. Today—next week—next month—what difference does it make?"

"But . . ."

"See, we like fightin'. Hell, we love it. We're real good at it or we'd be long dead. It's like, maybe, somethin' we gotta do. F'r instance, some fellas gotta be ministers. Well, we gotta be gunfighters." I thought the analogy a strange one, but didn't question it. Eddie paused again, this time for a full minute or so. "I guess that's why you don't see no ol' gunslingers. There's always some hothead kid who's a hair faster or a skinch more accurate."

"What about Dansworth's army?"

Dirty Eddie smiled. "Most of 'em ain't gunfighters, Jake. They're losers an' deserters an' cowards an' drunks. One-on-one, they ain't no more trouble'n swattin' a fly off your horse's ass. In a big group, some might get lucky an' take down a real gunfighter. Now, this Dansworth: I heard-tell about that pistol of his. Them grips ain't bone— they're ivory. The gunsmith who built the pistol, he's the absolute bes' in the entire West. An' the ol' gunman who taught him had some balls. Dansworth's good. He'd prob'ly take me. You—I dunno. I guess we'll see."

"Yeah. We will. Far's I know, ivory grips never won a gunfight."

We brought Teresa an' Blanca down to the barn about dusk. They weren't happy about it, but they didn't complain too much. Each of them clutched their rosaries. We set them up in the grain room with a lantern—there were no windows an' the only access to them was from the inside.

It was a decent night—some cloud cover, a half moon that shed some light, an' a tiny breeze that kind of poked around every so often.

Musta been close to midnight when we heard them coming.

"Madre mia!" Arm said. "Sounds like a stampede. Lotsa men, Jake."

Our men positioned themselves at windows an' up in the hayloft, sacks of .45 rounds and cases of 30.30 cartridges at their sides.

It *was* like a stampede—looked to be eighty or more men riding hard, spraying lead toward the house an' the barn. The first couple of torches smashed through windows of the house. The men who threw them were blown off their horses by our rifle fire.

The house caught fire good. I hated to see it go, but it was only minutes before long, hungry flames were reaching toward the sky and the interior was an orangish yellow inferno. The smoke was as thick as axle grease an' riders coming out of it looked like ghosts riding out of some battle that'd happened a long time ago.

If it hadn't been for the ear-shattering racket, the whole thing mighta been pretty like Fourth of July fireworks with muzzle flashes all over the place. But the roar of shotguns, the blasts of rifles, and the comparatively picayune reports of pistol fire destroyed any beauty there mighta been. The screams of the wounded an' dying, the pathetic squeals of wounded horses, an' that hideous rebel yell of the men who'd deserted the Confederacy, were like listening in on hell.

They came at the barn from both sides at first, but then shifted a cluster of men to the back. There was less smoke back there and our boys picked them off with almost ridiculous ease.

Dansworth gathered his troops on the far side of the burning house.

"They're gonna try a rush to the front," one of our guys said. "They got a lotta men, even if the sonsabitches can't shoot."

"Drop horses an' pick the bastids off onna ground," a voice from the hayloft called out. "We don't want that herd gettin' real close."

Arm an' I were at a window in front of the barn. Arm nudged me with his elbow. "Now?" I didn't need to answer. I stood an' the two of us hustled over to the cart, one on each side, and hauled back the tarp.

The Gatling gun stood there looking like a piece of some kinda farm machinery, 'cept for the barrel out in front. I shoved a couple of cases of cartridges outta the way an' half crouched behind the crank. All the barrels were loaded an' ready.

The enemy swept toward us like an insane wave of gunfire, bellows an' screams, an' smoke from our house. I truned the crank and fired maybe eight or ten rounds. It turned stiffly but smoothly and the blaze of fire from the barrel was almost blinding. I swung the whole thing to the left an' then began yanking on that crank. The clatter of the Gatling gun sucked in an' swallowed all the other sounds in the fight. Horses an' men went down like stalks of wheat cut by a sharp scythe. Arm kept loading and I kept firing.

It was a massacre, is what it was. But we hadn't gone to them—they'd come at us to take what was ours, to burn our house, to kill us all.

Some of them spun their horses to run but I kept on cranking. My right arm was cramping from pulling that handle, but I didn't give a damn. When I realized there was no return fire, I stopped. My face was burning from blowback an' both eyes were tearing to clear themselves. I ran my sleeve across my eyes and was able to see a bit better.

The ground between the house an' the barn was littered with dead men and dead horses. "*Jesús*," Arm breathed.

"We okay?" I shouted out, my voice a rasp in my throat.

We hadn't lost a man. I sat on a case of cartridges for a bit an' then pushed myself to my feet. My balance was a little screwed up an' my right arm felt like it'd been whacked with a bat.

"Lookit that," I said quietly to Armando.

"Ees too many dead, no? But the horses—they are ours, no?"

"They are ours—but . . . yeah, they're ours. We're entitled to keep what's ours."

"*Sí.*"

A few of our men moved out onto the battlefield and put bullets into the heads of those who weren't quite dead yet. I turned away. It was a mercy, of course—what the hell could we do for them? But putting a .45 into the skull of a man on the ground twisted my gut.

"Ees no other way."

"No," I agreed.

A voice echoed from next to our burning house.

"You and me—now. I shoulda blown your brains out the first time I saw you. I'm talking one-on-one—in front of the house. You got the balls to face me, Walters?"

I didn't bother to shout out an answer. Instead I walked past the Gatling gun and half the distance to the house. This, 'course, was dumb. Dansworth or any of his boys left alive could have put an end to me real easy. But, I'd thought about Dansworth an' I didn't think that'd happen. He was an arrogant l'il pissant—but he was good with that fancy .45 of his. I had a bit of a rep an' Dansworth wanted it. He walked out from next to the flaming house.

He had a cigar in his mouth, off to the side, an' he strolled as if he were going to a church meeting an' had plenty of time to get there. He looked real fancy; it was obvious that he gave the orders but wasn't involved in the battle.

"How many of those scum you had hiding her you lose?" Dansworth called.

"Not a one. An' you? How many of them losers you ride with can still walk?"

"Doesn't matter. There's lots of them looking for work."

"Coward work," I said. We were walking closer together.

Dansworth took a long draw on his cigar an' then tossed it aside. It bounced a couple of times and then lay there, smoldering.

"I hear you're pretty good," Dansworth said.

I didn't answer.

"I'm better. I'm going to kill you right here."

"Fine," I said. "Let's get to it, then. I gotta care to my mare an' colt."

Dansworth pulled an' then stopped, coughing. He spit a bit of blood at first, an' then it gushed out like water from a good pump. My round destroyed a bunch of his teeth an' kept on travelin'. Tell the truth, I don't remember drawin'—not exactly. I seen his fingers move an' I pulled an' fired, kinda crouched down, if he was faster'n me.

He wasn't.

The spigot of blood from Dansworth's mouth stopped after a couple seconds. So did everything else 'bout him. Arm came up next to me.

"Maybe now the Busted Thumb is okay? We can do the business we like, no?"

"Pard," I said, "let's go check our horses. All the gunfire mighta riled 'em some."

"*Sí*," Arm said.

Bill Pronzini & Marcia Muller

The dark clouds are gathering, and it's promising to be a doozy of a storm at the River Bend stage station ... where the owners are anxiously awaiting the return of their missing daughter. Where a young cowboy hopes to find safety from the rancher whose wife he's run away with. Where a Pinkerton agent has tracked the quarry he's been chasing for years. Thunder won't be the only thing exploding along ...

CRUCIFIXION RIVER

Bill Pronzini and Marcia Muller are a husband-wife writing team with numerous individual honors, including the Lifetime Achievement Award from the Private Eye Writers of America, the Grand Master Award from Mystery Writers of America, and the American Mystery Award. In addition to the Spur Award–winning title novella, this volume also contains stories featuring Bill Pronzini's famous "Nameless Detective" and Marcia Muller's highly popular Sharon McCone investigator.

ISBN 13: 978-0-8439-6341-0

Five-time Winner of the Spur Award

Will Henry

There is perhaps no outlaw of the Old West more notorious or legendary than Billy the Kid. And no author is better suited than Will Henry to tell the tale of the young gunman . . . and the mysterious stranger who changed his life.

Also included in this volume are two exciting novellas: "Santa Fe Passage" is the basis for the classic 1955 film of the same name. And "The Fourth Horseman" sets a rancher on the trail of a kidnapped young woman . . . while trying to survive a bloody range war.

A BULLET FOR BILLY THE KID

ISBN 13: 978-0-8439-6340-3

The Classic Film Collection

The Searchers by Alan LeMay

Hailed as one of the greatest American films, *The Searchers,* directed by John Ford and starring John Wayne, has had a direct influence on the works of Martin Scorsese, Steven Spielberg, and many others. Its gorgeous cinematic scope and deeply nuanced characters have proven timeless. And now available for the first time in decades is the powerful novel that inspired this iconic movie.

Destry Rides Again by Max Brand

Made in 1939, the Golden Year of Hollywood, *Destry Rides Again* helped launch Jimmy Stewart's career and made Marlene Dietrich an American icon. Now available for the first time in decades is the novel that inspired this much-loved movie.

The Man from Laramie by T. T. Flynn

In its original publication, *The Man from Laramie* had more than half a million copies in print. Shortly thereafter, it became one of the most recognized of the Anthony Mann/Jimmy Stewart collaborations, known for darker films with morally complex characters. Now the novel upon which this classic movie was based is once again available—for the first time in more than fifty years.

The Unforgiven by Alan LeMay

In this epic American novel, which served as the basis for the classic film directed by John Huston and starring Burt Lancaster and Audrey Hepburn, a family is torn apart when an old enemy starts a vicious rumor that sets the range aflame. Don't miss the powerful novel that inspired the film the *Motion Picture Herald* calls "an absorbing and compelling drama of epic proportions."

To order a book or to request a catalog call:
1-800-481-9191
Books are also available at your local bookstore, or you can check out our Web site **www.dorchesterpub.com**.

☐ **YES!**

Sign me up for the Leisure Western Book Club and send my FREE BOOKS! If I choose to stay in the club, I will pay only $14.00* each month, a savings of $9.96!

NAME: _____

ADDRESS: _____

TELEPHONE: _____

EMAIL: _____

☐ I want to pay by credit card.

☐ VISA   ☐ MasterCard   ☐ DISCOVER

ACCOUNT #: _____

EXPIRATION DATE: _____

SIGNATURE: _____

Mail this page along with $2.00 shipping and handling to:
Leisure Western Book Club
PO Box 6640
Wayne, PA 19087
Or fax (must include credit card information) to:
610-995-9274
You can also sign up online at **www.dorchesterpub.com**.
*Plus $2.00 for shipping. Offer open to residents of the U.S. and Canada only.
Canadian residents please call 1-800-481-9191 for pricing information.
If under 18, a parent or guardian must sign. Terms, prices and conditions subject to change. Subscription subject to acceptance. Dorchester Publishing reserves the right to reject any order or cancel any subscription.